PENGUIN BOOKS

EIGHTEEN AND WISER (NOT QUITE!)

Vibha Batra is a copywriter by profession and fiction writer by passion. Her literary pursuits took off when she translated her grandfather Late Shri Vishnu Kant Shastri's book on the Ishaavaasya Upanishad. Among her recent titles are *Sweet Sixteen (Yeah, Right!)* and *Seventeen And Done (You Bet!)*, published by Penguin, *Tongue in Cheek*, a collection of poetry, and *A Twist of Lime*, a collection of short stories.

To connect with Vibha and learn more about the book, please visit www.facebook.com/eighteenandwiser

Eighteen and Wiser
(Not quite!)

Vibha Batra

PENGUIN BOOKS

An imprint of Penguin Random House

PENGUIN BOOKS

USA | Canada | UK | Ireland | Australia
New Zealand | India | South Africa | China | Singapore

Penguin Books is part of the Penguin Random House group of companies
whose addresses can be found at global.penguinrandomhouse.com

Published by Penguin Random House India Pvt. Ltd
4th Floor, Capital Tower 1, MG Road,
Gurugram 122 002, Haryana, India

First published in Inked by Penguin Books India 2014

10 9 8 7 6 5 4 3 2

ISBN 9780143333197

Typeset in Perpetua by Eleven Arts, Delhi
Printed at Repro India Limited

www.penguin.co.in

For NBMP

Acknowledgements

On my DVD List:

For Babuji-Nani—*Angels in the Outfield*

For Mom-Dad—*Kabhi Khushi Kabhi Gham*

For my in-laws and extended family—*Meet the Parents*

For Meets, Mones, Teels—*Won't Back Down*

For SRS—*The Avengers*

For Sohini—*Partners in Crime*

For Nimmy and Team Penguin—*The Incredibles*

For all my readers—*Never Let Me Go*

For HP—*The Hurt Locker*

Chapter 1

Rinki Tripathi@ChennaiSuperChick
Hey, I'm on Twitter! About time too. I mean, even our PM's on it.

It was a regular Sunday at the Tripathi household.

Mom sidled up to Dad and cooed, 'Hey, that T-shirt looks so snug around your arms. Has someone been working out, hmmm?'

Dad didn't bother to look up from the newspaper he was reading. 'Sheena, please. We can't go to Express Avenue Mall every Sunday.'

'We don't do it *every* Sunday,' Mom pouted. 'Why, we ended up wasting all of last Sunday taking your old classmates on Chennai darshan.'

Dad lifted an eyebrow. 'Wasted? I distinctly remember you saying "My day is made" the minute you unwrapped the gift they brought for you.'

'Oh, the sari was fine. But what about the other important things in life?'

'You mean the matching petticoat and blouse?' Dad asked, his tongue firmly in cheek.

Mom shot him a frosty look.

'What I meant to say was . . .'

'I'm all ears, Sheena. What *did* you mean to say?'

'What about family time?' Mom said accusingly.

'What about it?' Dad shot back.

It was under these harmonious conditions that I landed on the scene.

I'd woken up early. By my standards, at any rate. And yet, there was a spring in my step, a bounce in my gait, a twinkle in my eye. With good reason.

It was the first weekend of my well-earned independence. The dreaded monster of the Board Exams had been laid to rest. The ghosts of my past had been exorcised. I was FREE.

In other words, I didn't have to stay up all night mugging. I didn't have to read thousand-page books that could single-handedly cure insomnia. My studying days were well and truly over. Yaaay!

It was only when Dad snorted that I realized I'd spoken aloud. I grabbed a newspaper and rolled it up. 'Morning, all you lovely people,' I spoke into the make-do mike.

'Maarning, maarning,' pat came the reply. From the most important person in our household—our domestic help, Rakamma.

If Mom was Munnabhai, Rakamma was Circuit. If Mom was Batman, Rakamma was Robin. (As Mom liked to say, 'Rakamma is my other half. After all, half my work is done by her.' To which Dad would rejoin, 'Just half?')

'How're we doing today, people?' I chirped merrily.

'I'm starving,' Mom declared.

'Er, Mom, it was a rhetorical question.'

'Then why did you ask it? Rakamma, where's my upma?'

'Guys, we have to talk. It's super important.'

'Hmm,' Dad mumbled, his nose settling deeper into the sports section.

Right then, Rakamma materialized with a plate of upma.

Great, just what I needed. On any given day, I have to fight for Mom's attention. But God help me when the rival is a plate of piping hot upma. Or crunchy masala vadas. Or crispy rava dosas.

I cleared my throat.

'So, what was I saying? Yeah! I'm a free bird! I AM A FREE BIRD.'

'Explains why you've been tweeting continuously,' Dad commented, pointing to his half-open laptop.

'Thanks, Dad, for derailing Chennai Express yet again—'

'Chennai Express?' Dad interjected. 'So you admit that you're a true blue Chennai-ite now? You're no longer Rajdhani Express? No more Dilli Billi?'

At that point, I almost lost my train of thought.

I held up a hand. 'Mom, Dad, give me a break. Do I interrupt you guys when you talk?'

'All the time,' Dad supplied.

Mom didn't look up from her plate of upma but her head bobbed vigorously. Hey, hadn't they been arguing just a few seconds back? Was that all it took to reunite them? And here I thought they were made of sterner stuff.

'Do I make fun of your ideas?' I continued. 'Do I refuse to take you seriously?'

'Yes, and yes,' Dad said, ticking my offences off his fingers.

'Sho whasch were you schaying?' Mom prodded.

'I was just schaying, I mean, saying . . .'

My makers looked at me about as encouragingly as a gambler would eye a losing bet.

'I have something to ask of you. Something that's very close to my heart.'

'Is this about that cell phone you want for your eighteenth birthday?'

Oh, hell. Was I making a mistake? Had I spoken too soon? Should I have saved *this* speech for *that* discussion? Too late. I was practically halfway into it.

'No, Dad,' I said, trying to sound as noble as I could. 'This isn't about a material possession. No matter how useful, how practical—'

'—how costly,' Dad remarked.

The conversation was costing me my patience.

'Guys, this is about an experience that I want to have.'

COUUUUUGHHHHH!

That was Mom choking. Dad reached out to pat her back. When she finally regained her composure, her mouth hung open in a big 'O'. As big as the portion she'd gobbled in haste.

Wait a second, whaaaatttt? Nooooo! Mom couldn't possibly be thinking of *that* experience. As if I'd ask her before having *that*. As if I had anyone around to have *that* with.

'Mom, Dad, I want to go to Delhi with my friends. For one whole week.'

There was pin drop silence in the room.

'May I please have one week of my life?' I beseeched.

'Didn't Kajol say that to Amrish Puri in *DDLJ*?' Mom whispered at last.

Dad shrugged. 'You're the movie expert, Sheena.'

I was talking about THE ONE thing that mattered to me and these people were discussing Bollywood technicalities?

'Guys, are you even listening?'

'Yes, Rinki, we are. Of course, you can go to Delhi—' Dad began.

Whaaaatttt? Dad was giving me the go-ahead? Just like that? It was like India giving Kashmir to Pakistan without a whimper. It was like SRK winning the Best Actor Award without being nominated. It was like Mrs Verghese (my ex-Princy and most vociferous critic) crowning me Student of the Year!

'—but on one condition.' And they say parents love their kids unconditionally.

'We'll come with you, too,' Dad finished. Finishing my hopes once and for all.

'Dad! How can I have fun with my friends if you both tag along?'

Dad raised an eyebrow.

'I mean, what will I tell my friends?' I hurriedly amended.

'First of all, it's not safe. Traipsing around an unknown city . . .'

'I've lived in Delhi for years!' I protested.

'What about accommodation? Don't tell me you were planning to stay in some *hotel*,' Mom said in horrified tones.

'We're planning to stay at Ankita's.'

'Who is "we"?'

'Robin, Sudha, me . . .'

'A bunch of young girls gallivanting around Delhi? It's just not safe. We cannot allow that.'

Okay, then. Here goes nothing.

'It's not just us girls,' I hurriedly put in. 'Google and Adit are coming, too.'

I just had to let the tomcats out of the bag. But what choice did I have? They were going on and on.

Mom gasped loudly. 'Those two boys again?'

I thought she'd be glad it wasn't a new set of boys each time. But clearly, I'd underestimated my folks.

'But they're my friends.'

'Admit that you like them, Rinki.'

'Of course, I like them, Mom. They're my *friends*.'

'Friends, my foot!' Mom railed.

'I'm just going out . . . er . . . going out of town with them.'

'Oh God!'

'Sheena, please. There's no need to get hysterical.'

'So now you want to send her to another city with a bunch of *boys*?'

'Sheena, relax. Rinki, listen. We trust you, we do.'

Mom's expression stated, 'I certainly don't.'

'But you cannot go to Delhi unchaperoned.'

My folks were taking the fun out of the whole thing. Really.

'Dad, I won't be unchaperoned. Ankita's parents will be there.' They were going out of town, actually. But he didn't need to know that.

Allow me to introduce you to my *Teen Survival Guide*—the survival kit for every fun-loving teen. **Rule #22**: When it comes to parents, all info must be shared on a strict need-to-know basis. Refer Jack Nicholson's epic dialogue from *A Few*

Good Men: 'You want the *truth*? Trust me, you can't handle the truth!'

'You can stay with Ankita. We'll stay with Mausiji. Unless, you want to stay with her as well?'

No chance in hell! Mausiji, Dad's maternal aunt, was a dreadful, frightful, trouble-breathing dragon. She'd paid us an extra-long, extra-controversial Nightmare-on Nungambakkam-type visit last year. Just thinking about it gave me the heebie-jeebies. Get this. I'd happily pull out every hair on my scalp than repeat the Mausiji experience. I'd sooner share a meal with Hannibal Lector than share a roof with her again.

I shook my head.

'Thought as much. What about the boys? Where will they be staying?'

At Ankita's, where else. But of course, I didn't say that out loud. I'd broken enough of my self-imposed rules already.

'Um, Google has some cousins in Delhi, Dad. The boys will shack up with them.'

Mom looked positively shacken, er, shaken.

'So it's settled. We're all going to Delhi. On that happy note, how about spending some family time together?' Dad suggested blithely.

'Family! That reminds me, the repeat of *Pavitra Pyaara Parivaar* is on,' Mom yelped, hastily reaching for the TV remote.

I was in a sea of white—white clouds, white mist, white light. I was dressed in Nirma white robes, and my skin, for once, was clear, translucent, glowing. A floral tiara graced my head. Glossy L'Oreal brown curls cascaded down my toned back.

Cute little cherubs played on oversized harps close by. There were giant platters of cupcakes, pastries, chocolates, French fries, vada paavs and samosas (I could eat them all without the fear of putting on weight). Hunky boys, all rippling biceps and six-pack abs, were fighting for their turn to feed me juicy black grapes.

You know that died-and-gone-to-the-big-spa-in-the-sky feeling? Well, that was my eighteenth birthday. In my dreams.

In reality? Not so much. In the words of my good friend Google, 'From young and stupid to old and stupid.' Adit, my other good friend, heartily agreed.

Never mind Google and Adit. They are such PPs, I tell you. Party Poopers. According to these boys, being eighteen is no biggie. I mean, heyloooooo! If wriggling out of your cage, breaking free from oppression, escaping the clutches of your captors isn't a big deal, I dunno what is.

Hey, I'm not saying that my parents are particularly impossible/non-understanding/tyrannical. Not at all. But they are PARENTS, for God's sake. And just how cool can parents be?

I mean, they may act all pally pally, promise that they 'get you', urge you to be 'open' with them. But when you finally let your guard down the teeniest bit, bam! All hell breaks loose.

As if there aren't bigger issues to get worked up about. I can think of a few right away:

1. My weight

2. Justin-Selena's relationship status
3. Katrina's wedding trousseau

Take it from me. Parents can only fall into the following categories:

1. Over-hyper and Over-controlling
2. Over-worried and Over-protective
3. Over-everything (dramatic/ambitious/zealous/indifferent/weird. Feel free to use the adjective that describes your parents best.)

Unfortunately, my parents fall into the last category. It's why I am the way I am. If only they belonged to any of the following categories:

1. Friendly and understanding
2. Relaxed and easy-going
3. Unquestioning and trusting

If only.

Take the biggest day of my life, for instance. I was going to have to lie to celebrate it. And by celebrate, I don't mean blowing a measly candle on a cake with your friends singing 'Happy Budday' off-key. Puhleeeeeze, I was a full-grown adult. And adults, as you know, have one and only one definition of 'celebrate': partayyyying hard.

After all, you are eighteen only once. Trust me, once you're old, you can botox and gym all you want, but you will always be *old*. Precisely why I wanted to bring in my eighteenth in style.

I had everything down pat. I'd be partying in Delhi. With all my closest friends. But you know what they say about plans (psst, they make God smirk).

Here's what happened. Dad couldn't take off right before my birthday. So the Delhi trip was postponed. Of course, my birthday couldn't be.

Good thing I had my *Teen Survival Guide* to turn to **Rule #28**. Always, always have a Plan B. And when faced with an extraordinary situation, it doesn't hurt to have a Plan C as well.

Rinki's Big B'day Bash (Plan A): Pardddyy in Delhi

Rinki's Big B'day Bash (Plan B): Rot, er, rock in Chennai

Movie Genre of the Week: Family

Rinki's Top 10

1. *Do Dooni Chaar*
2. *The Parent Trap*
3. *Amar Akbar Anthony*
4. *We Bought a Zoo*
5. *The Addam's Family*
6. *Kabhi Khushi Kabhi Gham*
7. *Stepmom*
8. *We Are Family*
9. *Bird Cage*
10. *Hum Saath Saath Hain*

Don't you just luuuurve movies? I zimbly heart 'em! They're so close to real life, no? I can totally relate to some of the characters. I mean, they could be moi!

Plus, after the Board Exams, I was the uncrowned president of the Vela Association, with nothing better to do than watch movies all day long. Only thing, I went about it in an organized fashion. I was like this serial killer systematically going after his victims. Week after week, I'd pick a genre, download or rent or borrow the best movies, and watch them religiously. It was movies, magic, masti all the way, yay!

Chapter 2

RinkiTripathi @ChennaiSuperChick
My parents' favourite 'F' word: Future. Don't even ask what's mine.

Robin, Sudha and I were over at Google's, browsing through his DVD collection.

'Hey, take this one. It's a murder mystery in which the gardener kills everyone,' Sudha said, plucking one enthusiastically.

I pulled a face. 'Thanks!'

'You can thank me after watching the movie,' Sudha said magnanimously.

'Watch this one. It's a real fun flick. A zombie infects the whole town and everyone pretty much dies in the end,' Google said, tossing a DVD at me.

'Sounds fun,' I said sarcastically.

Google paused from showing off his impressive collection. 'Talking of fun, my sis needs to be having some.'

'Having what?' Sudha asked.

'F-U-N,' Google spelt it out as if she was dumb or something. 'She's so depressed.'

'Boyfriend trouble?'

'Rinki, is that all you can think of? There are other things to be depressed about in life,' Robin said.

That I could totally agree with. The-Top-Five-Things-That-Depress-Me list popped into my head like a screaming advertising hoarding:

1. Weight issues
2. Parental problems
3. Insufficient pocket money
4. Lack of cell phone (in this day and age!)
5. Crazy hair

'Well, Neha's three years older than us. Worse, she's just passed out of college.'

'How is that worse, Googs? She's a college grad. Which means, she needn't study anymore. She can coolly turn around and say, "Bye bye books, ta ta studying." How can that possibly be a bad thing?' I wanted to know.

Google scratched his head. His way of saying, 'You've got a point there.'

'Well, she says it's official now. She's a grown-up. She can't fool around with her life anymore. Says if she screws up, Mom and Dad wouldn't let her get away with it,' Googs shrugged.

My eyes were round as saucers. 'There were letting her get away with things all this time? Sounds cool. Hey, can I trade my parents for yours?'

Google plopped down on the super-comfy La-Z-Boy. He worked the lever so he was in a reclining position—the favouritest position of all couch potatoes in the world.

'I think Neha's just worried. That's all. She'll have nothing to do, nowhere to go,' Google said.

'Why doesn't she get a job?' Robin said helpfully.

'A job!' Google chortled. 'Who in their right minds will give her a job?'

'Surely there's something she can do, something she is good at?' Robin insisted.

'I doubt it.'

See, this is the reason I don't miss having a sibling. I mean, siblings are supposed to be proud of you. To hero-worship you. As for criticism, ridicule, disapproval, well, that's what our relatives are for. Right that moment, Google was acting like a close relative.

'Neha doesn't want to join Dad's business. She doesn't like to do anything at home either,' he rattled on.

'Well, you certainly are coming clean with your sister's virtues,' I said sardonically.

'Maybe she should see an employment counsellor?' Robin suggested.

'Can't you see, Robin, she doesn't WANT to be employed?'

'Who doesn't want to be employed?' Neha asked, sweeping into the room in her nightclothes—a pair of checked pajamas and a pink T-shirt. She let out a huge just-got-out-of-bed yawn.

I sneaked a peek at my watch. Gosh, it was past noon. Hoo boy, Google's parents were reallllyyyy letting Neha get away with stuff. If I dare sleep that long, my parents would simply beat down the door. Even on Sundays. *Especially* on Sundays. After all, it happens to be Dad's day off. And god, is he watchful.

But weekdays are different. He's away at work. And Mom being Mom sometimes forgets she has a child sleeping past the deadline. But once she remembers, shudder! It's on to an eardrum-shattering bout of door pounding. I mean, I can still hear shrieks of 'Rinki, Rinkiiiiii, wake up' reverberating in my head sometimes.

'Rinki, Rinkiiiii, wake up!' Neha trilled, shaking me out of my reverie. 'I asked you a question. Who doesn't want to be employed?'

'Um, uh, it's someone Google knows. Why don't you tell her?' I said, narrowing my eyes at Google.

'Not important,' Google said glibly. 'So, Didi, what's up?'

'Don't call me that! I'm not Mamta Banerjee, okay?'

Robin smothered a giggle. 'So, what's up, Neha?' she enquired.

'Nothing much, Robin. Just that lately I've been feeling so old.'

Google looked as if he was about to say, 'But you *are* old.' One glance at Neha's face and he thought the better of it.

'C'mon, Neha,' I said kindly. 'You're not old.'

'I'm twenty-one,' she said morosely.

'My sister got married when she was twenty-one,' Sudha added by way of consolation.

I had to speak up. 'Umm, Neha, I really wish there was some way we could cheer you up.'

'Thanks, Rinki. But enough about me. What have you girls been up to?'

'Oh, nothing much. This and that,' I replied.

'Rinki's planning to throw the mother of all bashes,' Google began. 'Tell her about it, Rinks.'

'Oh! What's the occasion?' Neha enquired.

'Her birthday party. She's turning eighteen!' Robin and Sudha chorused.

Why did Google have to rub it in? The last thing I wanted to do was make Neha feel old. I glared at him.

However, it seemed to have the opposite effect on Neha. Her face split into a wide smile. 'Hey, I've a great idea.'

Now I was worried.

'Why don't we throw a joint birthday bash, Rinki?'

Loads of reasons, namely:

1. Because I didn't want to.
2. Because I wanted to hog all the limelight.
3. Because, much like toothbrushes, birthday parties are not meant to be shared.

'Oh, no, Neha! I wouldn't want to trouble you,' I said in saintly tones.

'Don't be so formal, Rinki.'

I wasn't being formal. Anything but.

'No trouble at all. It'll be fun! Trust me. So, where do we do this?' Neha asked, visibly excited.

I turned to Google, my eyes ablaze.

'How about our terrace?' Google replied, clearly mistaking the crazy gleam in my eyes for excitement.

'No!' I vetoed. 'How about renting out a beach house?'

'Awesome!' Neha said, rubbing her hands in glee. 'The theme?'

Two pairs of eyes turned to look at me. I'd turned into a zombie. I couldn't believe it was happening to me. It was supposed to be my big day. *My* big day. I felt like an American teen sentenced to prison on Prom Night.

'*Princess Diaries*,' I said, as if on auto mode.

'Woooow! I love that movie,' Neha exulted, clapping her hands in joy.

'It's actually a book adapted into a movie,' I corrected.

Even in the moment of grief, my inner perfectionist was alive and kicking.

'Oh, Rinki, tell me more.'

'We'll have a red carpet. We'll wear tiaras. Cute dresses with sashes. Ballerina flats.' I was like a mugpot vomiting all her knowledge during a verbal exam.

'Mind-blowing! What about the food? Wait, I've an idea.'

Oh God! Not another idea.

'Why don't we order pizza and garlic bread?' Neha squealed.

Pizza and garlic bread? What was she, a nitwit? I wanted to grab her by her skinny shoulders and shake her till all her bones rattled.

'Is that food befitting a princess?' I asked instead.

'How do you know what a princess eats?' Neha said stubbornly.

Because in my head I'm one.

'In the movie . . .' Neha continued.

'I know all about the movie,' I said dismissively. 'I've seen it ten times.'

'You were counting?' Neha asked in amazement.

I grit my teeth.

Google seemed to sense the tension in the air. He opened his mouth to speak. Good. A little support would be nice.

'She sure did. Rinki is crazy that way. If she likes something, she gets all obsessive about it,' he explained. Trust Google to light a match during inflammable conditions.

'Neha, we can't order pizza.'

'Why not? Look, I can understand that you want to avoid all those calories but . . .'

Like I needed any reminding.

'But come on, girl! It's your big day. You can diet another day. Let yourself loose.'

I wanted to let myself loose. On Neha. For crashing in on my party. MY PARTY.

'Go all out at the party, Rinki. Pig out, have fun!' She continued to dole out pearls of wisdom.

Well, I was trying to. Until you came into the picture, Neha.

'So venue, theme, food, done,' Google piped up. 'Let Rinki take care of the decor. She likes doing these things.'

'Great, thanks!' Neha crowed. 'Bye, girls! I'll go call everyone I know.'

'Goooooooooooooogleeeeeeeeee! I will kiiiiilllllllll you!' I bellowed the second she was out of the door.

Google held up his hands. 'I thought you wanted to cheer her up. I was just trying to help.'

'I don't need your help! Remember that the next time you open your big fat mouth. I just haaaaaate co-hosting parties. Hate it. Hate it. Hate it.'

Google looked genuinely surprised. 'You do?'

'Heyloooo, did you just meet me? I abhor it. I absolutely despise it.'

For a second Google looked as if he'd ask me what 'abhor' and 'despise' meant.

'But why?' was all he asked.

'Because . . . because . . .'

I bloody well couldn't tell him why. It would sound silly and stupid and selfish. And he wouldn't understand anyway. And even if by some chance he did, he wouldn't care. He wasn't a girl. He wasn't a party planner. He wasn't turning eighteen. Most importantly, he wasn't *me*.

'See? You're just being your usual compulsive self,' Robin said calmly.

So I was obsessive *and* compulsive. Great.

'Calm down, Rinks. It's going to be fun,' Sudha, ever the voice of optimism, predicted.

It wasn't.

It was the worst birthday party ever. I mean, ever.

The only good thing about it was the birthday gift. I'd told Mom and Dad ages ago: no mom-and-pop gift for my eighteenth. It had to be something big. Something special.

A special gift for a special birthday.

Obviously, there were only two candidates in the running. It was a toss-up between luscious locks and staying connected. Self-esteem or cell phone? Compliments or communication?

Needless to say, looks won. By a huge margin. I mean, I could always use the landline to call my friends.

Cool, right?

The conversation with Mom and Dad had been anything but.

Conversation between Mom-Dad and Rinki aka The Great Debate

I had waited one whole week before bringing it up. Realized they were never going to do it. So had no choice but to brazen it out.

I got a suitable opportunity one Friday night. Right after dinner. After all, everything sounds reasonable on a full stomach, right?

'So, any thoughts about the *near* future?' I asked Mom and Dad.

'Seeing as you just finished with your Boards, shouldn't we be asking you that question?' Dad said, his expression deadpan.

I never thought the Board Exam ghost would come back to haunt me long after it was dead and gone.

'I mean, any thoughts about my birthday gift?'

'Oh, that. I know just what to give my darling daughter . . .' Mom said grandly.

Trust me, Mom, you haven't a clue.

'. . . my black knitted poncho!' she finished triumphantly.

Gawd, not the black knitted poncho.

'You still have it? I thought you gave most of your stuff to Gangu Bai.' Mom had downloaded all her old clothes to the hired help back in Delhi before moving to Chennai two years ago.

'I did,' Mom nodded. 'But I saved the poncho just for you.'

Thank you, Mom. But I do not see myself as a caped crusader anytime soon.

'Mom, I can't wear the black knitted poncho. I'll melt in the heat.'

'You can wear it when you go to Delhi.'

'I hate the damn poncho.'

'But why, Rinki? It's soft and pretty. And it was in fashion until recently,' Mom insisted.

'It went out of fashion in 1947!' I cried out.

'Don't be silly. Just wear it and see. You'll be the envy of your friends.'

'I don't think so, Mom. Despite most of my friends being fashion challenged.'

'Fine, why don't you tell us what you want?' Mom said petulantly, crossing her arms over her chest.

Now we were talking!

'Let's see. I need a cell phone. I need to straighten my hair. I need a new dress. And accessories to go with it . . .'

'What happened to your old accessories?' Mom asked.

As if she'd ever wear an old petticoat and blouse with a new sari.

'Rinki, you don't *need* those things. You *want* them,' Dad said.

So there was a difference?

'Mom, Dad, please. Can we skip to the part where you just hand me the cash?'

'Or we can take it from the top,' Dad suggested mildly. 'You can tell us the ONE thing you really want on your birthday. And we'll see what we can do about it.'

Ah, they were going to play hardball. 'But Dad!' I protested.

'Rinki, you heard me. You've got more clothes than anyone I know,' Dad chided.

As if you've peeked into the cupboards of everyone you know.

'If you ask me, clothes are a sheer waste of money,' Mom clucked.

Yeah, right. That's why you bought that fluorescent green sari from Kumaran Silks just the other day.

'So what's it going to be, Rinki?'

I'd half a mind to yell 'nothing' and run out of the room. But then my folks are known to take things too literally.

'No rush. Take your time. Think about it. You can tell us over the weekend,' Dad said in soothing tones.

'No, no. I've thought about it. I really need to, er, want to straighten my hair.'

'Great then! Happy Hair Day to you!'

'Wait, you don't know how much it costs,' Mom said hurriedly.

Dad looked at me expectantly.

I couldn't bear to tell them the exact amount, so I reached for a pen on the centre table and scribbled it on the newspaper.

'My sari didn't cost half as much!' Mom yelped, her eyes round as buttons.

Hey, we were discussing a life-altering experience. And that doesn't come cheap.

'It costs as much at Bounce, Mom.'

Mom passed the paper to Dad. He sucked in his breath.

I was kind of confused. They knew it was my eighteenth, right? So why were they acting like that? Then I remembered. They were just being parents. My parents.

'Can't you get it done somewhere else? Some other parlour?'

Could Angelina wear anything but Dior, Prada, Armani on the red carpet? Could Bollywood flicks starring the Khans be expected to make less than 100 crores? Could our cricketers be persuaded to stop appearing in advertisements?

'Dad, I don't want to ruin my hair. I want to straighten it. Bounce is the safest. Bounce is the best.'

'Bounce is expensive,' Dad added.

'Dad, that's why I've been putting it off all these years. Because I didn't want to trouble you guys. Or overspend. Or feel guilty about overspending. I've waited and waited and waited. You asked me to study for the Boards, I studied . . .'

'Did she?' Mom asked Dad in a stage whisper.

'You asked me to cut down on my phone chats, I complied . . .'

'Her friends were too busy studying to take her calls,' Mom informed Dad.

I carried on as if I hadn't heard her.

'Now I'm asking you for something and you're turning me down?'

I was ready to cry now. Not those crocodile tears some kids shed to get their way. The real deal. Seriously, I just couldn't believe it. My parents were acting soooo tough. Hey, I never expected it to be easy. But I didn't quite expect it to be so hard either.

'Rinki, we didn't mean to make you cry,' Mom said softly, reaching for my hand. 'There, there.'

Mom wiggled her eyebrows at Dad like a seasoned Kathakali dancer.

'Er, Rinki, we're not turning you down. Not at all,' Dad acquiesced. 'Go to Bounce, get your hair straightened.'

Yipeeeee! I felt like running through the lawn sprinklers in my undergarments.

After all that hawing and hemming, they had finally came around. Classic Mom and Dad.

Movie Genre of the Week: Classics

Rinki's Top 10:
1. *The Wizard of Oz*
2. *Chupke Chupke*
3. *Gone with the Wind*
4. *Breakfast at Tiffany's*
5. *Casablanca*
6. *Bobby*
7. *The Godfather*
8. *Holiday*
9. *Sholay*
10. *Mughal-e-Azam*

Chapter 3.

Rinki Tripathi@ Chennai Super Chick
The best birthday gift in the world. The gift of choice aka hard cash.

Great hair. Check. Great outfit. Check. Great venue. Check.

The prelims were very much in order for the Princess' Ball. And right after lunch on D-Day, Googs and Neha picked me up and we zipped across to the beach house. I threw myself into work the second we landed there.

After a back-breaking hour, the place resembled a princess' frolic area. A recession-hit princess, if I may add. The co-hosts were conspicuous by their absence. But I didn't mind. With them out of the picture, I had complete control of the decor.

I scanned the party floor. Everything was in its place. Thank God. We were all set to rock, oh yeah. It was time to shine. Time to show all those school pass outs (my guests) and college grads (Neha's guests) how a party was thrown.

I bounded up the stairs. And bumped into Google on the way to the rooms. He was still wearing his faded white

T-shirt and printed shorts. There was a glass of Corona in his hand.

I mean, I just lost it. 'WHAT THE HELL! WHY AREN'T YOU DRESSED?'

'Thought I'd have a few pre-party drinks . . .' he gulped.

'GO, GET INTO THOSE CLOTHES!' I bellowed.

'On my way, Rinks, on my way.' Google shot into his room like Rajnikanth's redirected bullet.

Then came Neha's turn. In all fairness, I only meant to knock politely on her door. But I guess certain things are hardwired into our DNA.

Bang! Bang! Bang!

'Neha! Nehaaaaa! Open up! Let me in!' I hollered.

After a few agonizing seconds, the door swung open. I was zapped. Not only because Neha's blingy length dress was totally OTT. Over The Top. Think Lady Gaga meets Rakhi Sawant.

'Rinkiiiii, am sooo happy to see youuu, hic,' she slurred.

Gawd, what a couple of boozards, the brother-sister pair. I mean, who gets drunk at six in the evening? Stupid buffoons I'm crazy enough to co-host birthday parties with, that's who.

'Thankssss for coming to my party, Rinkiiii. You're shoo much better than Ajay.'

Seriously, Neha? *Your* party?

'He says something . . . hic . . . has come up at . . . work. He's always ditching me.'

Well, some of us have work to do.

With every ounce of self-control in my mind, I seized Neha by the shoulders. Propelled her towards a chair. 'Neha, why don't you sit here by the window? I'll help you pull on a pair of sheer leggings. Okay?'

'And . . . hic . . . and my drink?'

'Let me take care of that,' I said, plucking the long-stemmed wine glass from her hands.

'We'll pardyyyy, we'll dance, we'll sing,' Neha rambled while I rummaged through my bag. Hallelujah!

After restoring order, I hurriedly squeezed myself into a sleeveless black dress that (hopefully) hugged my curves in all the right places and ended just below my knees.

There was no time for foundation, concealer or blush. I'd have loved to go the whole hog: glitter on my eyelids, highlighter under my brow, shimmer powder on my arms. But but but. There was no frickin' time. Whatte pity. Not how I'd imagined getting ready for my birthday party.

I hurriedly lined my eyes with black liner, applied kohl on the inner rims, dabbed a bit of nude gloss on my lips, and sprayed a generous amount of perfume in Neha's direction.

'Here, let me help you up,' I said, walking into the fruity cloud.

We hobbled down the stairs. I plonked her into a plastic chair and fiddled with the controls of the music system.

'Hello, Princess!' Google said, making a grand entry. He was wearing a billowy white silk shirt with black trousers. He'd even gone so far as to gel his curls.

My face split into a broad smile. I ran up to him and linked my arm with his. Don't you just love it when people stick to the theme?

Soon, Robin, Sriram and Sudha were there. Hey, did I mention I'd helped them pick their outfits?

Robin was wearing a floral floor-length dress and low-heeled pumps. She had remembered to carry my beige clutch, I noticed with a touch of pride. And was that a coat of mascara on her lashes? Wowww. I was totally impressed. Love sure does great things to people.

Sriram was dressed in an off-white kurta pajama. He'd draped a tricolour stole around his shoulders. He looked more like a politician going for a press conference than a prince attending a soiree. But still. I was mighty touched. At least, my friends had made an effort. For my party. For me. Awww!

Sudha wasn't far behind. She'd teamed up a burgundy shift dress with my accessories—moon drop earrings, a metallic cuff and a long string of beads. If only she'd ditched the frumpy black shoes.

But I couldn't really fault her. Or any of my friends, for that matter. After all, I was the enlightened one. The Style Guru blowing cool mantras into their ears. They were mere kindergarteners learning their fashion ABCs.

'Hey, Rinki, your eyeliner's crooked,' Sudha pointed out.

Guess I'd been giving them way too many lessons.

'Girls, you look great!' I said selflessly.

'What can I say? Our stylist has done a fab job,' Robin smiled.

Ladies and gentlemen, presenting India's Stylist #1. Miss Rinki T.

'Rinki's too good, I say,' Sriram beamed. 'Many happy returns of the day, dear.'

'Thanks, Sriram. I'm so glad you could make it.'

I'd have loved to give him a hug but didn't want him to faint.

'Hey, where's Adit?'

'Here.' I swung around to meet him, eager to see the sartorial choices he'd made.

He was wearing a full-sleeve striped shirt and black trousers.

'Adit!' I chided him.

'Hey, I'm the common man. Your humble subject, Princess Rinki.'

'Well, if you put it that way,' I grinned.

'Hey, Rinks, here's your birthday gift. A little something from all of us,' Robin said, handing me a small white envelope.

So many contributors and a gift that fit into that little thing? Suddenly, I was worried.

'Lifestyle gift vouchers!' I exclaimed as I tore the envelope open.

The second best gift in the world. The beach house had just paid for itself.

'Thanks, guys! Love you all. Group hug?'

My wolf pack obliged happily.

The rest of the guests trickled in. Pity, the same couldn't be said about the rain.

I was about to offer Coke to Sudha when plop! A big raindrop fell into her glass.

'Eeeeeeeeeeeeeeeee!' I yelped, dropping the Coke bottle. I sprinted to the safety of shade. I'd blown megabucks on my new hair. I was damned if I let it go down the drain.

Sudha, Robin, Sriram and Adit followed suit. Neha and Google ran in the opposite direction.

Minutes ticked by. The rain continued to spray us lightly in the face. I twisted my hands over my head in a bizarre yoga-meets-umbrella gesture. I couldn't believe it. It was raining. In April. On the 22nd of April, to be precise. Bloody hell.

Robin looked around. The breeze swept two plastic bags in our direction. Nilgiris Department Store, the lettering proclaimed boldly.

'Here,' Robin said kindly, picking them up and pointing at my head.

Heylooo, I wouldn't use plastic bags for my groceries. And she was suggesting I wrap them around my head?

'Have it your way,' Robin sighed, releasing them into the wind.

Boom!

A loud clap of thunder sounded. Sudha lunged for Robin. I lunged for the plastic bags. The breeze had lifted them higher and I went sailing into the air like some despo fielder in a cricket match.

'Say cheese!' I looked up to see Adit pointing his phone at me.

I couldn't believe it. The hideous sight was imprinted on film forever. Princess Rinki securing ugly plastic bags on her regal head instead of a glittering tiara.

I would have swooped on to the offending cell and taken swift, merciless action. But it started pouring buckets. The guests began to run hither and thither, knocking down tables, kicking chairs out of the way. Soon, it morphed into a stampede-at-Kumbh Mela type of scene.

Only the kudikaars (Tamil slang for 'drunkards') Google and Neha remained unaffected. They continued to whirl in the rain, their eyes closed, arms outstretched. Proving beyond doubt that madness runs in the family.

What a way to bring in your big day. Sob!

Movie Genre of the Week: Tear-jerkers

Rinki's Top 10:

1. *Taare Zameen Par*
2. *Black*
3. *Rain Man*
4. *P.S. I Love You*
5. *Kal Ho Na Ho*
6. *My Sister's Keeper*
7. *Sleepless in Seattle*
8. *Schindler's List*
9. *Titanic*
10. *Never Let Me Go*

Chapter 4

Rinki Tripathi@ChennaiSuperChick
Best way to get over a boy? Another boy. Best way to get over a flop party? Hit holiday!

Yeah, so, my party was a complete dud. In the same league as *Tees Mar Khan, Kites, Himmatwala* (the remake).

Naturally, I was quite bummed. I cribbed to everyone who cared to listen. I whined and whined. I drowned my sorrows in cinema, chips and cake. But as a wise friend once said, 'Life goes on.'

On to the Delhi trip then. Ankita's parents were travelling to Maldives at the end of the month. Ergo, I timed the visit accordingly to get some alone time with my BFFs.

I had really wanted Robin and Sudha to come along too. But it was just me and the boys going to Delhi.

The girls ditched me. Or 'dropped out', as they delicately put it. But like Boyzone said in their unforgettable track, 'It's only words.' Sriram was in town only for a week. Translation: Robin couldn't bear to be away from him. Not four days out of seven.

Hey, doesn't distance make the heart grow fonder? I tried telling Robin as much.

When that didn't work I unleashed my 3 C Plan at her: Crib. Cajole. Condemn.

'I can't believe it. How can you do this to me, Robin? But you promised you'd come!' Crib.

'Robin, please come for three, okay two days. Please? You can bring Sriram along.' Cajole.

'That's an awful thing to do, Robin. How can you ditch your best friend for your boyfriend?' Condemn.

The 3 C Plan turned out to be a biiiig flop. Bigger than the comeback movies of Bollywood heroines.

Robin looked guilty as hell. But she didn't say 'Chalo Dilli'. Not once.

Sudha did. Several times. She wanted to come so bad. But she had a legit excuse. She didn't get permission from her parents. Well, they belonged to the same Let's-Torture-Our-Kids-For-No-Apparent-Reason league. See for yourself.

Parent Comparison Chart
aka
Who says the Taliban is in Afghanistan?

Rinki Tripathi's Parents	Sudha Balasubramaniam's Parents
Don't allow night stays.	Night stays allowed. But only at Robin's. (And more recently, Rinki's.)

(Cont.)

Rinki Tripathi's Parents	Sudha Balasubramaniam's Parents
Frown upon late nights. Late night as in anything after 9 p.m.	Frown upon late nights. Unless she is accompanied by Robin. (I bet Robin's family ration card had Sudha's picture, too.)
Permit dresses, knee-length skirts, spaghetti tops (preferably with a shrug thrown on top).	Sleeveless tops are a no-no. Spaghetti tops are banned. Knee-length dresses can be worn on occasion. With leggings, of course.
Aren't okay with me owning a cell phone.	Only just bought Sudha a cell phone
Happily sent me to the parlour on my birthday.	Happily sent Sudha to the temple on hers.

In a nutshell: Expecting them to let Sudha go to Delhi was like expecting a socialite to wear the last season's dress to Lakme India Fashion Week.

Poor thing. Unlike me, Sudha didn't have any relatives or friends up North, so she couldn't even jump on that bandwagon.

Google and Adit, of course, had no such problems. Because they were boys. Harrumph.

Sometimes, just sometimes, I wish I were a boy. All that freedom! All those choices! But then sanity prevails. I think of their limited clothing options and go, 'Thanks but no thanks.'

In the end, I'd no choice but to go to Delhi with my folks.

The boys were going to fly in the same evening. Giving me a whole afternoon to spend with Ankita.

She picked me up from the airport. Thank God. Or else my parents would've insisted on depositing me at Ankita's place. I mean, we could get so much stuff out of the way right in her car.

Need I add our reunion was just like the proverbial Bharat Milaap (you know, where Lord Ram meets his bro Bharat after ages, tight hugs follow and . . . oh, just read those epics).

'Anksssss!!!!' I screamed. 'Ohmmyyyygosh, you look so good!'

Anks looked smashing in her cherry-red skinny denims and ruffled white top.

'I know, right! You don't look so bad yourself, Rinks! I luuuuurrvee the hair.'

I pirouetted for her benefit. *Swish! Swish! Swish!*

'Thanks, Anks,' I chirped.

'Uncle, Aunty, so good to see you!'

'Good to see you, too, Ankita. Have fun, girls,' Mom waved at us. There was a company car waiting. She and Dad got into it and sped away.

'So, my love or should I say "lau", what's the POA?' Ankita asked me.

Plan of Action? Well, I had it all chalked out.

'I want to pick up coloured denims. Bottle green, candy pink and neon blue just like . . .'

' . . . the Princess of Wales,' Ankita and I said in unison.

We could still finish each other's sentences. God, I'd missed her!

'I want to pick up a dress from Zara . . .'

Ankita threw my bags in the boot of her car.

'First things first. Bhaiya, bar chalo,' she told the chauffeur.

'This time of the day?' I yelped, scrambling in after her.

'Nail Bar, Rinks, Nail Bar.'

Oh!

Cut to Nailorama.

I brought Ankita up to speed with my life. An uncensored, unedited, unvarnished account of The Life and Times of Rinki T.

'. . . that's all about me. What about you, Anks? What have you been up to? Tell me everything.'

'Nothing much, Rinks. Same old boy troubles. Where have all the good guys gone?'

I remembered something Google had told me not so long ago. 'Maybe you're being too picky?'

'Nah! A well-dressed, well-travelled, well-mannered boy. That's all I want. Is that too much to ask?'

Hmmmm. She kind of missed the 'well-heeled' part.

'Surely you've come across a few guys who fit the bill?'

'Yup, they seemed all right in the beginning. But in the end, they turned out to be such losers. I think I'm done,' Ankita declared, holding up her sparkling nails to the light.

'With boys?' I asked her.

'No, silly. My nails. But maybe you have a point. Maybe I should go off boys for a while.'

Made sense. I do the same thing. With non-veg. Every now and then, I give it up. Not for too long, say a week or so. And then, when I go back to my mutton kebabs and chicken tikkas, sluuurp! I enjoy them more than ever.

Rinki's *Teen Survival Guide* **Rule #53**: Give up something briefly to get more fun out of it.

'What say, Rinks? Should I take a break?'

'If that's what you want,' I ventured carefully.

Ankita Khanna is a great girl and all. But she is kind of nuts. She gets all these weird ideas, gets really gung-ho about them, and then just as soon, pfft. They go bust. And when that happens, it's not a pleasant sight. Probably because Ankita's busy blaming everyone in sight. Which is why I never want to be part of her decision-making process. Ever.

'But what do you think?' Ankita insisted.

'I think we're getting really late,' I said, neatly deflecting the subject. 'We better get home.'

'Let's go to Big Chill first.'

Ankita had made an offer I couldn't possibly refuse.

It was late evening by the time we got to Ankita's place. I hurried up to her room to freshen up.

The doorbell rang shrilly.

They were here! Google and Adit were here! My dream holiday with my friends was about to take off.

I dashed down the stairs to receive them.

Too late. Ankita had already done the honours.

'Welcome home, boys! You have curly hair, you must be Google,' she said, enveloping him in a hug.

'And you, you are wearing specs. So you must be Adit,' she said, ignoring his outstretched hand, throwing her hands around him.

'She's good,' Google told me with a grin.

Elementary, dear Watson.

'Hi Google, hi Adit,' I said, with a lame wave.

Adit looked distinctly uncomfortable. I should have warned Ankita. But the girl's so friendly!

'What can I get you to drink?' Ankita asked Google.

I wanted to say, 'Hey, they just got here.' But I guess she was just trying to be a good host.

'I'll have a beer.'

'Beer? Why?'

'What do you mean "why"?' I spoke up for Google.

'Come on, Google. You can do better than beer,' Ankita coaxed him.

'Anks, he must be tired . . .'

'No, no, I'm not tired,' Google said gallantly. 'I'll have what you're having.'

Ankita rewarded him with a devilish grin. 'Now we're talking. Try this raspberry vodka. Topped up with Sprite.'

Google accepted it with reverence.

I bristled. Last time someone offered him a vodka, he'd called it a 'ladies' drink'. Incidentally, that 'someone' happened to be me. And now he was acting as if he was being conferred a doctorate by some prestigious American university.

Ankita turned to Adit. 'What about you?'

Oh, this was going to be fun. Adit was a die-hard teetotaller. He'd sooner have poison than an alcoholic beverage.

'Nothing for me, Ankita. Thanks.'

'He doesn't drink,' I told her.

'Well, why don't you have a Breezer? It has only 4 per cent alcohol,' Ankita persisted.

Oh, only 4 per cent. That made it what? Non-alcoholic?

'No thanks, Ankita. I'm fine.'

'Have some Coke, Adit,' I said helpfully.

'Come on, Adit. You can have Coke in Chennai. You're in Delhi now. Have a Breezer. Have some fun.'

Adit stood there stiffly, an undecided expression on his face.

'Well, okay,' he said, caving in.

My jaw dropped to the floor. WTF? I flew to his side.

'Adit! What are you doing?'

'I'm not doing anything.'

'You're drinking! You don't drink.'

'It's just a Breezer. It has only 4 per cent alcohol.'

'Adit,' I began calmly. 'Are you feeling okay?'

Ankita looked from me to Adit and back to me. 'Hey, Rinks, are *you* feeling okay?'

'I've toh never been better, baba,' Google said gleefully, fully enjoying the *tamasha*.

'Here, pass it to Adit,' Ankita said, handing me the requested drink.

I closed my fingers around the bottle. 'No! I'm not going to pass it to Adit. Not until he tells me what's going on.'

'I'm an adult, Rinki. I can do as I please. I can drink what I want.'

'No! You've to drink what I want,' I blurted without thinking.

'What the hell is wrong with you, Rinki?' Ankita snapped.

'I'm sorry for sounding like your mother, Adit but . . .'

'Actually, Rinks, you're sounding like *your* mother,' Ankita interjected.

God, no!

'If the boy wants to drink, let him drink,' Ankita hissed.

'Listen to the lady,' Google drawled from the couch.

What could I do? I was heavily outnumbered. I gave up.

'So, where do we go tonight?' Ankita asked.

'Why don't we party at home?' I countered.

'Don't be boring, Rinks.'

'Yes, Rinks, don't be,' Google said teasingly. I wanted to whack him.

I waited for Ankita to ask Adit. Back in the day, he would have wanted to stay home. But he'd started drinking. No saying what he'd do next.

'Let's not hang out anywhere close to home. I know this great pub at Gurgaon. Or we could even go to this awesome nightclub in Saket.'

'Cool,' Adit said, leaving me flabbergasted once again.

Perhaps the shock of the Board Exams getting over was too much for him.

'You're the expert,' Google told Ankita, an 'I'm lovin' it' expression on his face.

Tch tch. One day in the capital and the boys had already imbibed the *chamcha* culture.

A good hour later, we were in the car. I was in the passenger seat. The boys were at the back, with Ankita squashed in between. I still don't know how *that* happened.

'Rinki, play Radio Mirchi.'

The latest Bollywood chartbuster blared out.

'How far is Gurgaon from GK, Bhaiya?' Adit asked the chauffeur after an hour.

'With this kind of traffic, two hours at least,' Ankita supplied.

'Two hours? We could go from Chennai to Pondicherry in that time,' Google said in horror.

'Well, you aren't in Chennai anymore. Aren't you glad?' Ankita smiled.

I wasn't. I wanted to be in the backseat. Where all the action (and I don't mean that kind of action) was. I felt so cut off in the front seat. As if I was travelling alone to some remote part of the country.

'Can't we go some place closer home? In GK?'

'Bhaiya, *gadi modo*. Urban Pind chalo.'

The chauffeur turned the car.

'I've always wanted to go to a dhaaba,' Adit said softly. 'One of those authentic ones, you know.'

'I know a great place on the Delhi-Jaipur highway,' Ankita piped up.

'Jaipur.' Google shuddered.

'Are you sure, Anks? Is it safe and all?' I said, a trifle uneasily. After all, Delhi was not just the food capital of the country. It was also the crime capital.

Driverji answered on her behalf. 'When Laakhan Bhaiyijj here, havve no phear.'

'Chill, we'll be there in a jiff,' Anks beamed.

We weren't.

It was worth it, though. It was like those dhaabas you see in Bollywood movies. Deserted. Dilapidated. Decidedly in the middle of nowhere. Lit by the glow of kerosene lamps. With a couple of charpoys strewn around carelessly.

We went and plonked ourselves on one of them. An elderly Sardarji was stirring a big pot in the ramshackle hut that housed the kitchen. His younger counterpart was busy serving the other table. Two burly truck drivers were going at the grub with admirable gusto.

Google flailed his arms wildly and succeeded in catching our young steward's attention.

'One murgh tikka, three naans, one black daal, one butter chicken masala, one chola pindi, two Cokes,' Google rasped.

The rest of us were about to nod in approval when he added, 'That should do for me. Guys, don't waste time, tell him what you want quickly.'

Adit and I flicked Google in the back of his head.

'*Jaldi*, please! Okay, Sardarji? Very very *bhooka*,' Google implored him the second we had placed our order.

Young Sardarji clicked his fingers to connote the time it'd take.

Alas, he was exaggerating. The food took a while coming but when it did . . . we leapt at it like we'd been kept on a Karwa Chauth fast all week.

In the meantime, our fellow guests pushed the plates back, and staggered to their feet. They wiped their hands on their moustaches, burped heartily, and coolly started making their way to the truck without clearing the tab.

'Oyyyyyyyeeee!!!' the elderly Sardarji called out after them.

The truck drivers wilfully ignored the chef's impassioned plea and quickened their pace.

Three pairs of eyes followed the unfolding drama with bated breath. I clutched Ankita's hand. Her other hand tightened over the steel tumbler. Adit's hand was about to pick up a piece of murgh tikka; it froze in mid-action.

Google seemed to have gone in to big time france (a food inspired trance). All through the commotion, his eyes didn't leave the plate, not even for a nanosecond. With enviable focus, single-minded determination and loud chomps, he went at the succulent chicken tikkas, pausing only to lick his fingers.

Suddenly, who should come bounding out of the kitchen but the Young Sardarji, brandishing a hockey stick over his head, a fierce expression on his face.

Without so much as a backward glance, the freeloaders broke into a run. Within seconds, they reached the truck door and yanked it open. In quick succession, they swung their legs up and heaved themselves in, and disappeared into the cavernous interiors.

'Aaaaaaeeeeeeeeeeeeeeeeeeee!' Young Sardarji let out a blood-curdling cry and came hurtling in our direction.

Right then, Google happened to jerk his head up. His hand shot up in eager anticipation. 'One more butter chicken masala, Sardarji.' He punctuated the sentence with a loud burp.

In response, Young Sardarji hurled the hockey stick with all his might at the retreating truck.

The next day, a nightmare woke me up. I saw Mom dialling my number a dozen times. It was so vivid. I actually saw 112 missed calls on Ankita's cell phone screen.

I reached over a sleeping Ankita and grabbed her cell phone from the night stand. Gosh, it was noon! I hurriedly dialled Mom's number. We couldn't have her 'dropping by' now, could we?

She answered on the first ring. Worse, she sounded super tense. I hastened to assure her I was fine. She said Dad was busy at work and she was going shopping. Surprise, Surprise.

Although the dhaaba dhishoom-dhishoom had provided us enough thrills to last a lifetime, I was determined not to let Day Two pass in a blur.

I went about waking up the lazy lumps of lard . . . Mom style, I'm afraid. With her trademark loud bangs on the door.

Mission accomplished, I padded into the huge, airy kitchen. I flopped down on one of the high chairs at the breakfast counter.

'Some coffee for you, Adit?' Ankita asked.

'Or is there something else you'd like to drink?' I added sweetly.

'Coffee sounds great,' Adit said, flashing Ankita his special smile.

Excusez moi! Why on earth was he flashing *her* that smile? Hadn't *we* been out on two dates? Dates that involved devouring idlis at six in the morning, the little voice in my head reminded me.

I know, I know. It wasn't as if he was my boyfriend. We weren't going steady. Or anything like that. But still. He'd no business awarding newly minted acquaintances with *that* smile.

'Are you going to make it?' Adit asked Ankita.

I almost choked on my chocolate milk. Anks? Make

coffee? The only thing Ankita could make in the kitchen was a mess. Her domestic skills were worse than mine. Believe it or faint.

'Of course not! Bidya Aunty!' she called out.

Bidya Aunty materialized.

'Two cups of coffee, please, Aunty,' Ankita said. Turning to Adit she asked, 'Have it the way I like it?'

Adit nodded, the corners of his mouth lifting.

I was *so* glad they were talking about coffee.

'Morning, people!' Google said, bursting into the dining area. 'Morning, Ankita.'

'Morning, Google. Sleep well?'

'Like a baby,' Google said, flashing her *his* special smile.

Crap! At the cost of sounding repetitive, Google and I had been on two dates. Two dates that involved devouring sandwiches. Shut up, you stupid little voice in the head. All my dates involved polishing off large quantities of food. So? It didn't prove anything.

Weren't you the one who told Google it wasn't exclusive, the Little Voice of Woe persisted. Oh, so it was okay for Google to ogle my best friend? I don't think so.

Flashback time. I was dating Google and Adit. At the same time. I'd had the courtesy of keeping them both in the loop. Long story short, they weren't too thrilled about it. Google had sulked for weeks. Adit had aired his discomfort. Neither had asked me out again.

After that the Board Exams happened. The End. Sure, we hung out together. But to take a leaf out of FB, my relationship status with the boys was 'Complicated'. To say the least.

'What's for breakfast?' Google asked Ankita.

'Omelette, bacon, ham, toast, muesli, yogurt, orange juice.'

'Wow, did you read my mind?' Google said in admiration.

I was glad they couldn't read mine.

'Okay, after breakfast, we'll go for a little sightseeing trip. It's your first time in Delhi, right Adit?'

Sightseeing? What was this, an SOTC group tour?

Adit nodded.

'Hey, my second cousins live here. So I've been to Delhi a couple of times. But I don't mind seeing it from new eyes,' Google piped up.

Ugh! Somebody kill me.

'Great! Here's the itinerary. Red Fort, Qutub Minar, Purana Qila, Jantar Mantar, Chandni Chowk.'

'But Anks, the boys'll get so bored with this long-winded Delhi Darshan.'

Confession: I'd get bored.

'I think it'll be interesting,' Adit countered.

Did he *have* to contradict every little thing I said?

'What do you suggest we do, Rinks?' Ankita asked. She knew what I was going to suggest.

'Why don't we go shopping?' I said happily. Coming to Delhi and not going to a mall would be like going to a temple and not seeing the deity.

'And the boys won't get bored with that?' Ankita said, tossing them a say-it-isn't-so look.

The boys, however, were waiting for an opportunity to cast their votes in her favour.

Sigh.

Day Two was sacrificed in the interest of history.

'Let's go home, order pizzas, and yak through the night,' Ankita chirped on the way back home.

'Street fight! Street fight!' Google suddenly raised an alarm. Our eyes followed his pointing finger. Sure enough, an irate motorcyclist was aiming well-aimed punches at a tempo driver. 'That right there, that's Delhi's biggest tourist attraction.'

Delhi had certainly lived up to its reputation.

Much to Ankita's chagrin, so did the Chennaites. By the time we reached home, we could hardly stand straight. And sadly, drinks had nothing to do with it.

Day Three, we caught up at the breakfast counter again. Ankita was busy reeling off instructions to her battalion of hired help.

'Had a good time yesterday, guys?' I couldn't help asking them.

They looked so tired, so beat, so washed out. Sightseeing still sounds like a great idea, hmm, boys?

'It was . . .' Adit paused to consider the word.

'Educational?' I needled.

'Fun,' he said at last. Adit and the rest of the world had different definitions of the word. Clearly.

'My ass it was fun,' Google raged. 'Six hours of being stuck in traffic. Seven hours of melting in the sun. All this for what? To stare at some old crumbly buildings?'

I smothered a grin. 'Er, Google, those old buildings? They're called monuments. Delhi's filled with them.'

'You mean there are more?' Google's eyes widened in horror.

'What? Don't you want to play Archaeology Archaeology today?' I asked sweetly.

'More like Aarghh-eology Aarghh-eology,' Google muttered. 'Rinki, please save me!'

Hey, in those fairy tales, wasn't it the prince who rescued the damsel?

'Fear not, Google. Today, we shall explore other man-made wonders. Like malls.'

'I like malls,' Google said, letting out a sigh of relief. 'They're air-conditioned.'

'Someone save *me*,' Adit groaned.

If it was up to me . . . Ankita swept in with a hearty, 'I'm here, Adit.'

And who asked her to volunteer for the job?

'Thanks, Anks. Glad I can count on you.'

I think I puked a little bit in my mouth.

We reached the Emporio-Promenade-Ambience mall cluster in Vasant Kunj shortly after lunch.

'Hate to sound like a country bumpkin but this is cool!' I gushed.

'Forget cool, it's bloody awesome! I didn't know India had malls like these,' Google enthused.

Adit had a 'I don't know what malls are like and I don't want to know' expression on his face.

We trooped in. I was excited. Not just because I was going to shop. I couldn't wait for the boys to observe Ankita in her natural habitat. They were treating her as this

Outstation Goddess. As someone who was uber cool. But they didn't know the first thing about her. She could be bossy, stubborn, impatient. Often times, all at once. AND she was a shopaholic.

'Follow me, everyone,' Ankita muttered.

True to form, Ankita went on rampage. Designer tees, check. Designer heels, check. Designer shades, check. Designer bag, check.

'Hey, I didn't know there were so many luxury brands available in India,' Google said admiringly.

'I didn't know there were so many luxury brands,' Adit rejoined.

I made a beeline for Zara. A gorgeous peach dress with lace and net trimmings called out to me. And I just had to answer its call.

In my defence, it was just one measly dress. It managed to burn a huge hole in my pocket though.

Ankita's pockets, however, ran wayyy deeper.

We followed her around, checking every price tag religiously.

By the end of the shopping expedition, Adit and Google had invented their very own code lingo.

Shake of the head—Frightfully expensive, dude

Eyebrows raised—Couldn't afford it even if I sold myself, bro

Soft whistle—F@#$, I've seen diamonds that cost less

Hand on mouth—Now-you've-got-to-be-bloody-shitting-me

Slapping forehead—Man, I could buy a plot in Chennai with this

While they'd been conversing in Morse code, she'd been shopping with no remorse code.

'Gosh, Rinki. She's worse than you,' Google commented, as Ankita emerged from the Chanel store, carrying a little souvenir.

Finally. The compliment I was waiting for.

And after she handed her eleventh shopping bag to Adit, even he had to agree with the statement.

I was sooooooo happy. It was a good day for friendship.

And for the tummy. To make amends for her excesses, Ankita treated us to some divine pasta at Auma, the swank Italian restaurant at the mall. Like Googs told his folks over the phone later that evening, Mummy, it was yummy.

Chapter 5

RinkiTripathi@ChennaiSuperChick
Caesar was lucky. He had only one Brutus in his life.

Most people get homesick. I, on the other hand, just get sick of home. But a funny thing happened during this trip. I actually felt happy at the thought of going back to Chennai. Had I gone from Snotty Northie to Fun Madrasan without even realizing it?

'What's up for the day, Anks?' Google asked warily, half afraid to hear the answer.

'House party!' Anks replied, throwing her hands up in the air. 'BYOB. CAYAP.'

Google's expression said 'What crap!'

'Bring Your Own Booze, Come As You Are Party,' I explained. Google relaxed visibly.

'Not a very big party, I hope,' Adit asked hopefully.

'No, no, just a couple of our old classmates.'

It was Adit's turn to relax.

In the end, it was a couple of our old classmates, their boyfriends, their friends and their girlfriends. Half of Delhi,

I think. Ankita had called everyone at seven. Of course, everyone was on Indian Standard time.

The first batch of my old classmates arrived at nine.

'Megha, Jiya, Kavita! So good to see you all,' I said, kissing the air near their ears.

My fake smile was firmly in place. Matched only by their fake smiles.

'So, liking Chennai or what?' Megha asked, a pitying expression in her eyes.

'Oh, I luuurve Chennai. It's so cool . . .'

'Are we talking about Chennai?' Google asked, barging into the conversation. 'It's nothing compared to Delhi. Dilli is where the action is at.' He jabbed his fist at an imaginary opponent.

'Girls, have you met Google?' I said, ever the loyal wingman.

'Google? What kind of a name is that?'

'Short for Goga?' Kavita asked.

Babe, we don't have names like that Down South.

'Short for Jugal,' he explained.

'How is that short?' Megha wanted to know. 'Jugal is five letters. J-U-G-A-L. Google is six.'

A big round of applause for Megha's mathematical skills.

'Long story,' Google began, whisking them aside.

More ex-classmates trooped in. More PC (polite conversation) happened. I was getting bored to tears when a group of seriously good-looking boys entered.

I got to my feet. Megha, Jiya and Kavita went running to them. 'You guys are late.'

Even those losers had boyfriends, I sulked, retreating into a corner.

Adit was taking shelter there as well.

'Some madhouse, huh?'

He shrugged and took a swig of his Bacardi Breezer.

That reminded me. 'Adit, we need to talk.'

'Now, Rinki?'

'Yes, now.'

'What about?'

'About you. What's going on, Adit? You're drinking? You are actually drinking? Are you depressed?'

'Hey, aren't you always asking me to stop being so serious? Telling me to have fun?'

'So this is your way of having fun, Adit?'

'Maybe. Like yours is dating two guys at once.'

Ouch! I should have known it would come back to bite me in the ass.

'Oh, so that's what's bugging you! Why didn't you say anything then, Adit?'

Things had been pretty awkward, what with Google raving and ranting. So I was kind of relieved when Adit played Mr Strong and Silent. Stoooopid bloody optimism.

'Does it matter, Rinks?' He took a longish swig from the Breezer bottle. Talk about bottling your feelings.

'It does.'

'Hey, what're you quarrelling about?' Ankita said, appearing on the scene.

Adit and I glared at each other.

'Break it up, you two! Come on, let's rock this party.'

Ankita dragged me away. But not before I shot Adit a severe 'this discussion's so not over' look.

The lights had been dimmed. There was a makeshift dance floor. The latest chartbusters blared out of the speakers. My feet tried to keep up with the bhangra tracks.

A steady stream of people poured in. By midnight, Ankita's house was jam-packed with strangers, some of whom were running around, waving their T-shirts over their heads Sourav Ganguly style and screaming at the top of their lungs.

Through the smoke, I spotted Google some distance away. I hurried over to him.

'Having fun?' I yelled in his ear.

'Yeah, yeah! But tell me something. Why do people in the North all dance the same way?' Googled yelled back.

He cupped his right hand and bobbed it up and down. 'Fix the light bulb, fix the tap,' he yelled, mimicking the moves of the enthu hordes on the dance floor.

Googs was such a hoot!

Right then, Vineet, who was doubling up as the DJ, dared to play a track by a notorious Punjabi rapper known for his misogynistic lyrics, only to be hotly booed down by the girls.

'I better get him to play something cooler,' Google muttered, scooting off.

Sure enough, 'Ippidi podu podu podu' came on full blast. Google ran to the middle of the dance floor and whooped in delight. He pretended to fold his imaginary lungi to his knees and began belting out some really energetic 'koothu' moves. Leaving Google to regale the audience with the local dance of our home state, I slipped away.

My feet were KILLING me. I needed to find a place to sit. ASAP. I stumbled across the room, my eyes hunting for the couch. Had some idiot moved it? No, it was right there. It was now covered by one big person. I peered. Oh, it was couple in a passionate lip lock.

I was about to walk away but then the guy came up for air. He reached for the Breezer bottle and took a longish swig. As if he was drawing courage from it. I froze. That gesture, that bottle. It was Adit. *He* was kissing? He *was* kissing! A girl that wasn't me! In my agitation, I took a couple of steps back. And banged into the exquisite Ming vase right behind me.

Chinggg went the vase as it swayed violently.

The girl in question jumped and whirled around.

Gasp! Adit hadn't just been kissing any girl. He'd been kissing Ankita!

Adit looked up right then. Even though the lights were dim, I couldn't bear looking at him. I turned on my heel.

'Rinki!' Adit and Ankita called out at once.

'You okay?' they chorused as I ran into a pillar.

I'm fine, guys, don't stop on my account. I just need a minute. To puke my guts out.

I ran down the length of the living room, right up to the stairs. And straight to the washroom. I locked myself in. My heart was hammering away in my chest.

Too muckin' fuch. Adit and Ankita. Ankita and Adit. Making out. I would have never ever believed it. But I'd seen it with my own two eyes.

Oh, why didn't I go blind before seeing that? Bollywood movies don't exaggerate. Suddenly, they made complete sense to me.

Despite myself, I was half-hoping they'd followed me. To offer some sort of explanation. There had to be, just had to be, one.

1. Plausible Explanation

Adit: 'Sorry, Rinki. I mistook Ankita for you.'

2. Feasible Explanation

Ankita: 'Sorry, Rinki. I couldn't really see in the dark. Adit and my ex are the same height.'

3. Bearable Explanation

Adit and Ankita: 'Sorry, Rinki. It didn't mean anything. We were both sloshed. We didn't know what we were doing.'

4. Intolerable Explanation

Adit and Ankita: 'Well, we kind of like each other. Good thing you saw what you saw. We didn't know how to break it to you.'

I ran into the bedroom, locked the door behind me and threw myself on the bed. A couple of hours later, the jagrata party dispersed. The house went silent. I tiptoed out of the room. Put an ear out for footsteps.

Perhaps Ankita would come knocking then. Try to apologize. Try make up with me. But after a while, I heard the door to the next room open and close. Ankita'd probably decided to crash in her parents' room. I resigned myself to the fact that I'd be spending my last night in Delhi miserable and alone.

Try as I might, I couldn't sleep. My mind was racing. What was going on? Did they really have the hots for each other? Since when? More importantly, how come? They had nothing in common. As if you have anything in common with Adit, whispered the idiotic little voice in my head.

I didn't sleep a wink the whole night. Early next morning, I dragged myself out of bed. Took a quick shower, threw my clothes into the suitcase and went out of the room. Maybe, just maybe, I could leave before anyone woke up.

Unlike me, they'd be in no rush. I was on the noon flight with Mom and Dad. Google and Adit were taking the evening flight back to Chennai.

'Rinks,' came Ankita's voice behind me.

I jumped out of my skin.

'Shit!' I said, clutching my top. 'You scared me.'

'Sorry, Rinks,' Ankita whispered, drawing closer, throwing her arms around me.

She wasn't saying sorry for startling the daylights out of me.

I disengaged myself from her embrace.

'Hey, you're up early,' I said in the overly-enthusiastic tones I usually reserve for relatives, acquaintances and strangers.

'I couldn't sleep,' Ankita said, her voice small.

'Too much to drink.'

It wasn't a question.

'Too much to think, Rinks.'

I held my breath. Please God, let it not be Explanation #4. Anything but Explanation #4. I could deal with anything but that.

'I didn't mean to hurt you, Rinki.' It was going to be Explanation #4.

'What on earth are you talking about, Anks?' I said whirling around.

'Rinki, wait. Don't walk away. Hear me out.'

I was scared to. I didn't want to hear how great Adit thought she was. Or how madly he'd fallen in love with her. Or how superior she was compared to me. I didn't want to hear anything. I just wanted to go home.

'I knew you guys weren't exclusive . . .' Ankita said.

I cursed myself for telling her that. Then another terrifying thought struck me. Had Adit been talking to her too? Discussing our stupid history? Spilling the beans on our little misadventure? Jerk!

'I thought it wasn't going anywhere,' Ankita continued.

'Neither is this conversation, Ankita,' I said brightly. 'I'm cool. Don't worry about it.'

I tugged at my suitcase.

'Wait, I'll ask someone to carry it out to the car.'

Ankita called out for her staff. The chauffeur appeared. We followed him down in silence.

'Byeeeee, Ankita,' I sang out, clambering into the car.

'Rinks, hang on a sec. Why don't I come with you till your aunt's place? We can chat on the way . . .'

I cut her off mid-sentence. 'Hey, you have guests to take care of, remember? Don't want you to be a bad host.'

I slammed the door shut. The car sped away leaving a wretched-looking Ankita behind.

I didn't utter a squeak all the way to the airport. Mom put it down to 'Poor thing. She's missing her friends and Delhi already.' Dad insisted, 'She's probably sad that her holiday is over.' That made me sadder still.

Mom and Dad didn't know me at all. But still, they'd never ever hurt me in the horrifying way my friends had.

Movie Genre of the Week: Horror

Rinki's Top 10:

1. *The Grudge*
2. *The Ring*
3. *The Shining*
4. *Psycho*
5. *Bhoot*
6. *The Blair Witch Project*
7. *Exorcist*
8. *The Evil Dead*
9. *Raaz 2*
10. *Paranormal Activity*

Chapter 6

Rinki Tripathi@ChennaiSuperChick
The thing I like best about Delhi? The Exit gate at the domestic airport.

Present day: May first week
College opening: June last week
Time in hand: Seven weeks

I don't know who was getting more bugged about the above. My parents or me.

I mean, Dad had started lecturing me on 'Time Management' right from the time we boarded the Delhi-Chennai flight. So I did what anyone would do under similar circumstances. I tuned out.

I guess this is what Dad must have said:

What are you doing with your life?
It's time **to** make some tough decisions.
Don't let your hobbies **eat** into your time.
Oh Rinki, the time to act is **now**.

But this is what I heard:

What ....

................**to**........................

.... **eat**..............

....**now**...............

Back in Chennai, things went from bad to 'very worst'. Mom-Dad were after me like tax collectors after a stash of black money.

What next? Which course? Which college? *Think, Rinki, think.* (If my Dad were a Bollywood producer, that's what he'd title my launch movie.)

Don't waste time. (Me, waste time? Nevah!)

Do something productive. (Like you need a college degree to do that.)

Go to bed early. (Hell, no!)

Wake up early. (Little DIY advice: sleep at half past two and try it next morning.)

Do something other than watching movies, browsing on the laptop, listening to music and chatting with friends. (Basically, everything that makes me happy.)

OMG, stop already, I wanted to scream. It was the first half of the holidays. First half, sob. How much more refined would the torture get?

As if the AA, that is, Adit-Ankita hounding wasn't enough.

Ankita buzzed me on the landline every single day. I hung up on her every single day. Adit messaged me a couple of times on FB. I hit delete even before reading the messages. Okay, right after reading the messages. 'Can we meet? Would like to talk. Call me.'

Google called, too, and gave a blow-by-blow account of the party. Apparently, there was an altercation on the dance floor. Over a girl, what else. Cuss words had been traded. There was some pushing and shoving. Beer bottles had been broken. Sigh. That's the problem with Delhi. Uncalled-for aggression. In Chennai (and the rest of the country), we pick up a bottle from its bottom. In Delhi, people begin by grabbing its neck.

And oh, Robin and Sudha dropped by, eager to hear all about Delhi. I couldn't think of a single charitable thing to say about it.

When it was their turn, all they could talk about was, you guessed it, the future.

Robin's Short-Term Goal: Get admission in Chennai Women's College. Course: B.Com.
Sudha's Short-Term Goal: Copy paste above.
Rinki's Short-Term Goal: Park my ass somewhere, anywhere, for the next three years.

Knowing Robin, I bet she'd mapped out the next hundred and fifteen years of her life. For herself and Sudha. Had I given her the chance, she'd have gladly done that for me. But I wasn't going to hand over the reins of my life to anyone. Not to my parents. Not to my friends. Not to destiny.

I was going to take charge. Grab life by its balls, um, in a manner of speaking. Go from crappy day-ums to Carpe Diem. I resolved to go about things in an organized manner. I did have a commerce background, after all.

First things first. The college.

According to the general public, Chennai had some good colleges. By good, they did not mean cool. Just academically sound. Yawn!

Future Calling Rinki Tripathi

PART I

Operation Alma Mater

Step One: Zero in on college.

Options: Ethiraj, MOP Vaishnav, Chennai Women's College (CWC).

Preference: Can a common man dictate terms to a politician? Can a flop Bollywood actor afford to throw tantrums? But if you still want a preference, fine, it was CWC. (MOP had a very strict dress code. No skinny jeans, no tight tees, no short tops. So what was I supposed to do, donate the contents of my wardrobe to charity? Ethi had impossible cut-offs. Hey, a girl's got to be realistic.)

Strategy: Apply in all, get in one.

PART II

Target Academic Course

Step one: Decide on the course.

Options: B.Com, BBM, BBA, BA Economics.

Preference: B.Com

Plan of Action: Keep fingers crossed, make occasional temple visits, offer regular prayers.

I put my pen and paper away. See? It had taken me all of one afternoon. My future was set. I knew what I'd to do with my life. Mom and Dad had been worrying not just endlessly but also needlessly.

There was just one thing left to do: put the Ankita-Adit episode behind me. It was hounding me in my sleep. It was bugging me every waking hour. I was tired of thinking about it. I just had to get it out of my system. Once and for all. I needed to be gainfully employed. But where?

I zeroed in on the place quite by accident. Neha, bless her, forwarded me something. On most days, I condemned all forwards to trash. But I was so bored, I actually read the whole thing.

Turned out, it was an ad for a slogan writing contest at *Divaa*, Chennai's leading lifestyle magazine. Neha thought it was just up my street. The first prize caught my eye. A month-long internship at the magazine.

Writing slogans? Hmmm. Several sprang to mind:

Fresh rahoge, pyaar milega
Thodi pagalpanti bhi zaruri hai
Aaj kuch toofani karte hain

I mean, how tough could *that* be? I used to write stuff like that when I was in second grade.

I went through the ad again in excitement, my mind working furiously. Once I got a foot in the door, I could always get the job I wanted. Junior Stylist at *Divaa*. The current stylist was someone called Lokeshwari aka Loki. Her claim to fame? 'I love fashion.' But evidently, fashion didn't love her back.

It sounded perfect. I was made for the job. I could totally do it. Better than Lokeshwari, at any rate.

At the end of the hour, I'm proud to say I'd outdone myself. If any of those ad agency types had seen the slogans, they would have hired me on the spot. Oh, yeah.

Divaa's Slogan Writing Contest

Complete the following sentences as creatively as you can and who knows, you could become *Divaa*'s next slogan writer! Go on, get cracking!

I'm a Divaa in real life because.............

Divaa is Chennai's favourite because......

Rinki's Entries

I'm a Divaa in real life because if life is a cola, I'm the fizz. Oh yeah, I like to say it like it is.

Divaa is Chennai's favourite because be it fashion, style, glamour, Divaa sets the pace, leaving every other magazine behind in the race.

You know, I'm not like those bookworms who claim they haven't done well in a exam only to score centum in it. The minute I hit the 'sent' button, I *knew*. I'd knocked the slogan contest ball right out of the frickin' park.

Sure enough, in a week's time, I received a mail from them saying I'd won and could I please send my resume across. Sure could! Yoooohooooooo!

Google Search: Sample resumes

Resume

Name	Rinki Tripathi
Date of Birth	22.04.1994
Residential Address	Flat 3D, Tulip Apartments, 16 Nungambakkam High Road, Chennai 600034
Contact Number	044 28330202/cell number pending*
E-mail	rinkirocks@gmail.com
Educational Qualifications	XII grade—Chennai Bal Vidya Bhawan. Percentage pending.
Work Experience	Organized school farewells and culturals Planned and executed many successful parties for family and friends Wrote a very popular blog in school
Languages Known	Hindi, English, working knowledge of Tamil*
Hobbies	Reading books and fashion magazines, watching movies, listening to music, chatting with friends, eating out, styling people, dancing
Special Skills	Dealing with difficult people, soothing ruffled feathers, giving makeovers

All the above particulars are true to my knowledge.

Rinki Tripathi

*Like Joey said in an episode of Friends, 'Hey, everybody lies on their resume, okay.'

Movie Genre of the Week: Adventure

Rinki's Top 10:
1. *Indiana Jones and the Last Crusade*
2. *The Mummy*
3. *The Great Escape*
4. *Indiana Jones and Raiders of the Lost Ark*
5. *The Good, The Bad, and the Ugly*
6. *Inglourious Basterds*
7. *Dances with Wolves*
8. *Zindagi Na Milegi Dobara*
9. *Dil Chahta Hai*
10. *The Mummy Returns*

Chapter 7

Rinki Tripathi @ChennaiSuperChick
Say hello to a proud member of the Indian Work Force.

It was official. I wasn't *vela* anymore.

I had a job! A real job! Yipppeee!

I wanted to shout it out from the snowy tops of mountains. I wanted to mount a loudspeaker on a cycle rickshaw and announce it to the world. I wanted to hire a little Cessna and write it all over the sky.

Since all the above activities were *slightly* over my budget, I did the next best thing. I summoned an EFM. Another one of those Emergency Family Meetings.

There we were, huddling on the newly upholstered couch. Dad looked relieved. I'd saved him from yet another dull afternoon at Express Avenue Mall.

Mom, on the other hand, looked like a rubber band, stretched to breaking point. She acted that way before every single EFM I convened. As if her worst fears were about to get confirmed.

As if I was about to toss my modesty to the wind and declare 'Yes, yes, yes, I'm:

1. Druggy
2. Preggy
3. Tipsy
4. All the above'

Well, Mom was wrong. On all counts.

'Mom, Dad, there's something I want to share with you.'

'Make it quick, Rinki,' Mom cut in, clutching her stomach, her face a mixture of anxiety and fear.

'Please, Sheena. Let Rinki talk,' Dad admonished her.

'There's good news,' I began brightly.

I was looking at Dad. I really didn't want to miss the expression on his face when I dropped the bomb. So I didn't quite notice Mom's features rearranging themselves rapidly.

'There's a new development in my life. Something big,' I said, patting my stomach. Gosh, I could hardly keep the news to myself.

Mom's horror-struck eyes followed the movement of my hand.

'You may not want it for me right now . . .'

Mom gasped. In hindsight, this would've been a good time to look in Mom's direction.

'You may even ask me to reconsider but I've made up my mind . . .'

'Noooooooooooo!' Mom burst out, unable to hear another word.

'What?'

I was shocked. Mom had a problem? With my job? My first ever job. A job I'd landed on my own steam.

'Rinki, how could you?' Mom cried out.

'What do you mean, Mom? The way everyone does!'

'Sheena, Rinki—' Dad began.

But our heated exchange drowned out the voice of reason.

'Mom, if anything, you should be proud of me.'

'Proud?' Mom railed. 'You want me to be proud of you?'

'Yeah, Mom, proud! You certainly didn't seem to mind it when my cousins got one.'

'That was different. They got one AFTER they were married,' Mom spat out.

'What difference does it make?' I cried out. 'I thought you'd be happy, happy your daughter was all grown up. That she finally got a job . . .'

'J-j-job?' Mom repeated slowly, as if she was hearing me for the first time.

Now, wait a minute. WHAT was Mom thinking?

'That's what she said, Sheena,' Dad put in mildly.

'You've got a *job*?'

'Exactly what Rinki's been trying to tell you for the last few minutes,' Dad said in exasperation.

'*You've* got a job?'

All that emphasis on different words. Gawd, I was beginning to get seriously pissed off.

'Yes, Mom. So sorry not to disappoint.'

'But where?' Dad asked.

'And how? I didn't know you were good at anything,' Mom added.

Now, isn't that something every child wants to hear?

'What Mom's trying to say is you've never displayed any interest in working,' Dad said soothingly.

Ladies and gentlemen, allow me to introduce you to my makers. Ever the believers of my talent.

'Who gives jobs to school pass-outs?' Mom wondered aloud.

I reached for the centre table, grabbed a magazine, and waved it with a flourish. 'That's who!'

'So you'll be delivering magazines door to door?' Mom queried.

Tch, Mom's faith in me was touching.

'Mom, Dad, meet the juniormost slogan writer at *Divaa*, Chennai's leading lifestyle magazine!'

'Slogan writer? I thought you wanted to be a stylist? So you've realized that you need to be stylish to be one,' Mom sighed.

Seriously. With parents like these, I just don't know how I've come so far in life.

'You don't even like bright colours,' Mom added by way of explanation.

I do like bright colours, Mom. But not when you wear them all at the same time.

'Back to what I was saying, guys,' I said out loud. 'I've got a job! A real job! Isn't that exciting?'

'It certainly is,' Dad agreed. 'But what about the pay?'

Uh, oh.

'Umm, the pay, well . . .' I trailed off.

Dad leaned forward.

Damn. He wasn't expecting the exact figure, was he?

'I'm not sure about the amount, Dad.'

'But Rinki, you should be. It's important to discuss these things beforehand. You don't want to jump into anything only to realize you're being ripped off, right?'

Too late for that now.

'Yeah, absolutely, Dad. I made it absolutely clear to them. Told them that the pay better be good or else.'

Not really.

'But still, Rinki. It's best to have these things on paper. Have you signed a contract with them?'

All I wanted to sign was a non-cooperation contract with my parents. Why did they have to sound so sceptical? Why did they have to ask so many questions? Why did they have to spoil everything? Why couldn't they just be happy for me?

'Um, I'm not sure, Dad. I'll keep you posted. Okay? Now, I better go and tell my friends.'

'I always knew it was a good idea to have her,' Mom said while I was still within earshot.

Gee, thanks.

'Everyone said I was spoiling her rotten, encouraging all that fashion nonsense . . .'

They did? Grrr!

'But my Rinki's proved everyone wrong.'

Suddenly, I wasn't so sure anymore.

I reached for Dad's laptop and updated my FB status. Then came the turn of Mom's Blackberry Messenger. The screen lit up the second I was done.

'Congrats,' Adit texted.

I'd half a mind to delete it. But then I thought the better of it. Hey, I was the star of the moment. It was time to gloat.

'Thanks,' I messaged back.

'I'm so proud of you, Rinki.' What was he, a mother hen?

'Rinki? You there?'

'Yeah.'

'Can we talk?'

'We are talking.'

'I mean, can I call you? Now? You've been avoiding my calls.'

'Wrong! I've been avoiding you, Adit.'

'But why?'

'You know why!'

'Because I hooked up with Ankita?' Adit texted.

Because you should have checked with me before doing so.

'But Rinki, you said we could date other people. That we weren't going steady.'

That didn't mean you could kiss the first girl you came across, I wanted to scream.

'That didn't mean you could kiss my best friend Ankita,' I texted instead.

'But you were seeing our mutual friend Google,' Adit insisted.

Surely that was allowed? Because it was, well, me.

'Rinki? You there?'

'Would you stop asking that? I'm here, Adit.'

'Then why don't you say something?'

'What do you want me to say?'

'Say what you're thinking, Rinki.'

'I think you and Ankita are making a big mistake. This casual dating stuff is not for everyone.'

'But we're not thinking of dating casually.'

I let out a sigh of relief.

'We're thinking of going steady.'

Whaaaaaat? Blooody hell!

'I feel that's the only way to make things work. Otherwise, it all gets messed up.'

The way it happened in our case. Adit didn't type that. But I knew that's precisely what he wanted to say.

Gosh, my head was reeling.

'Rinki, you there? Say something.'

What did he want me to say? Adit, I'm very happy for you and Ankita. Now please, just go to hell.

'Adit, Mom's calling. I've got to go. Bye.'

I scrolled up and read and reread the conversation a dozen times. Only then did I hit the 'End chat' button. I wanted to delete him as well, from my BBM contact list. But I couldn't bring myself to do it. How else would I read his status updates/snoop on him and Ankita?

Adit and Ankita. Adit and Ankita! It was really happening. I wouldn't have believed it. Not in a million years. I mean, they were like tea and ketchup, pasta and curd, tandoori chicken and coconut chutney. They just didn't go together.

It was enough to drive anyone crazy. Then I remembered. I had a job. To be more specific, a non-paying internship. But still. At the cost of sounding like my Dad, it was time to think of the future. The future was calling. Loud and clear.

Movie Genre of the Week: Futuristic

Rinki's Top 10:

1. *ET*
2. *Inception*
3. All *X-Men* movies
4. All *Transformer* movies
5. *Mr India*
6. *Robot*
7. *Krrish*
8. *Koi Mil Gaya*
9. *Back to the Future*
10. All *Terminator* movies

Chapter 8

Rinki Tripathi @ChennaiSuperChick
'Why should boys have all the fun?' goes a bike ad. I want to know what's *so* fun about riding a damn bike?

I broke the news to Robin and Sudha at Café Coffee Day.

'Guys, I've some good news.'

'Got a new dress?' Robin asked archly.

Robin could be such a spoilsport, you know.

'No, it's something bigger than that,' I said happily.

'What could be bigger than a new dress?' Robin said coolly. 'Let me see, a new dress *and* new shoes?'

'Shut up, Robin! I've got a job!'

'Congraaaaaats, Rinki!' Sudha exclaimed, jumping to her feet. She hurtled in my direction and threw her entire weight on me, crushing ribs and bones in the process.

'Oh, it's nothing, Suds,' I said modestly.

'Come on, Rinks, admit it. You're thrilled as hell,' Robin said wryly.

'Oh, well! A little, I suppose.'

'Liar,' Robin laughed. 'Tell us more.'

'Ladies, you are looking at *Divaa*'s new slogan writer.'

'Wow! I love *Divaa* magazine. I take my style tips from them,' Sudha said excitedly.

Oh, really? Here I thought she took all her style tips from *me*.

'It's a Monday through Friday thing,' I went on.

'It does sound cool,' Robin conceded. 'It's right up your street. But tell me, Rinks, have you really thought this thing through?'

I'd done little else over the last week. Oh yeah, I had everything covered. All it took? Couple of lists, couple of tables, and that's it. I was set, game, match.

Day of the Week	Outfit of the Day
Monday	Leggings and tunic
Tuesday	Trousers and full sleeve shirt
Wednesday	Long skirt and sleeveless top
Thursday	Jeggings and long kurtas
Friday	Dark blue denims and short kurtis

Day of the Week	Packed meal of the Day
Monday	Chicken sandwich
Tuesday	Chicken kathi roll
Wednesday	Idli podi
Thursday	Egg noodles
Friday	Chilly cheese toast

See?

I shared my Success at Work blueprint with Robin.

'Well, you forgot about the most important thing,' Robin replied.

What could be more important than clothes and food?

'Conveyance,' Robin said, making me feel like a fully-dressed person on a nudist beach.

'Oh, noooo! I'm so screwed!' I wailed. I'd completely forgotten about that.

Ever bought a gorgeous dress and realized you didn't have the shoes to go with it? Ever signed up for swimming lessons and realized you didn't own a swimsuit? Ever gone for a movie and realized you forgot to wear your contact lenses? Good, so you know how I felt.

How the hell would I get to my place of work? Public transport was out of the question. The buses were the playground of all Roadside Romeos. Eww! And you could take autos only if you were Richie Rich. Groan!

'Perhaps your dad could drop you?' Sudha suggested.

'My dad leaves for work before I wake up,' I said ruefully.

'He could be persuaded to leave late,' Robin said.

'Yeah, and cannibals could be persuaded to turn vegan,' I retorted.

'You could try leaving early?'

'Leave early and do what? Sweep the floor in office? Work starts only by elevenish.'

The table fell silent.

'You're right, Rinki,' Sudha said at last. 'You're screwed.'

'Now, now, Rinks, don't lose heart. Tell you what, you can always get a bike.'

'A bike! Chance *illa*! I'm so not going to ride a bike!'

'But why?' Robin persisted. 'Bikes are convenient, efficient, affordable . . .'

'. . . and dangerous,' I said with a shudder. 'I was in a bike accident as a child. Never wanted to go near one after that.'

'But . . .' Robin opened her mouth.

'I'm not going to ride a bike,' I said firmly, signalling the end of the discussion.

'Fine, Rinks, as you wish. Where is your office, by the way?'

'Sterling Road.'

'That's not too far from where you stay. It's just ten minutes from Nungambakkam. Perhaps you can walk?'

'At eleven in the morning? I don't think so, Robin. I'll get fried in the sun.'

It was Agninakshatram or the hottest time of the year in Chennai. The crazy hot and fiery month of May. Well, I had no interest in giving such a big agnipareeksha. Trial by fire, guys. Most kids grow up listening to nursery rhymes. Courtesy Mom, I grew up listening to the epics.

'You mean, you'll get tanned,' Robin said dryly.

Oh, well. That too.

'Okay, how about this? I can pick you up on the way to the gym. But you'll still get tanned riding pillion . . .'

'Ohmyyyygosssh!' It was my turn to hurtle across the room and envelop Robin in a bear hug. 'You'd do that for me, Robin? Really? Gosh, you're my bestest friend in the world.'

And that made me a tiny bit sad. Not so long ago, Ankita had that honour. Look how *that* had turned out.

'Hey Robin, what about me?' Sudha squealed.

Uh-oh. Robin and Sudha went to the gym together. On most days, at least. On days Robin was feeling lazy, Sudha had no choice but to bunk.

Owning a bike could be a good thing sometimes, I had to grudgingly admit.

'Here's the plan, Rinks. I'll leave home at ten thirty, pick up Sudha, then pick you up. I'll drop you off to office, then go to the gym with Sudha. We'll work out for two hours and pick you up on the way back. Cool?'

I couldn't stop myself from giving my personal Wonder Woman another rib-and-bone-crushing hug.

Genre of the Week: Superhero Movies

Rinki's Top Ten:

1. *Batman Begins*
2. *The Dark Knight*
3. *The Dark Knight Rises*
4. *The Return of Superman*
5. *Spiderman*
6. *The Avengers*
7. *Thor*
8. *Captain America*
9. *Iron Man*
10. *Iron Man 2*

Chapter 9

Rinki Tripathi@ ChennaiSuperChick
Vroooom! Vroooom! Yours truly, a biker chick. Who would have thought?

It wasn't cool. As we discovered the very next day.

We were out for a 'dry run', as Robin called it. A practice session on her bike. Robin was at the helm, I was squashed in the middle, and Sudha brought up the rear. Trust me, my butt did not thank me for that. I wondered how Ajay, Arshad, Tushar and Co. had done it in the *Golmaal* series.

To make matters worse, at the very first intersection, we were flagged down by a cop.

Robin slowed down dutifully.

'What, Saar,' she asked, as she parked at the side of the road.

'Going trippies, aa?'

'Saar, short distance only.'

'Naat allowed, you know?'

'Naat know,' I spoke up, thoroughly peeved.

It was ridiculous. We were just three broke girls going on a bike. We weren't breaking any laws. We weren't going over the speed limit, much less over sleeping pavement dwellers. That's all cops could do. Arrest girls for updating their FB status, accost them for going trippies. Grrrrr!

'Er, Rinks, I'll take care of this,' Robin said, shooting me a quelling look.

'It is against the "laa". You know?'

Oh, so going trippies was against the law? And auto drivers fleecing passengers mercilessly was not?

'No, I do naat know,' I said mulishly.

'Rinki, puhlllleze.' This time it was Sudha.

'Saar, sorry. Mistake. I'll drop her right at the end of the road,' Robin said, pointing at me.

'Very danger trippies, you know?'

'Naat know,' I said again.

'Very worst habit, you know?'

'Naat know,' I insisted.

'Rinki!' Robin and Sudha chorused.

I was so bugged. I just swung one leg over the bike and jumped on the pavement.

'Saar, I have to go,' Robin pleaded with the cop.

'Vokay, vokay. Next time doing means fine.'

The cop swatted us away.

I started walking on the pavement. Robin and Sudha trailed me on the bike.

'Rinki, I'm so sorry.' Robin flapped her feet like a hapless penguin in a bid to keep up with me.

'Not half as sorry as I am,' I muttered.

'Guess this trippies thing is not going to work out,' Sudha said sadly.

Talk about stating the obvious.

'Tell you what, Rinks. You get a bike and I'll give you riding lessons,' Robin offered.

No way in hell!

'Robin, start the bike. Just go home please.'

We were beginning to draw strange looks from the passersby.

'I'm fine, trust me. I just need some time to think. Why don't we meet at my place this evening?'

'Are you sure?' Robin asked.

I nodded. Home was barely five minutes away. I waved at the girls and started walking.

It was time to weigh the options.

Pros of Working:

Getting to do what I loved doing—writing and, eventually, styling

Getting tons of experience, which would come in handy after college

Getting out of home every day till college started

Getting to do something other than think about Adit and Ankita

Cons of Working:

No pay
No transport

I scrutinized the ratio. 4:2. Hmmm. I just had to find a way out of my predicament. But what?

Perhaps I could impress the magazine guys with my hard work, dedication and skills. Show them how exceptionally talented I was so they would insist on paying me? Or I could tell them my sob story and they'd take pity and make it a paid internship. Hey, it was just for a couple of months. Surely they could afford one measly grand or two?

Divaa's office was housed on the topmost storey of a modest commercial apartment. There was a bank on the first floor and a travel agency on the second. Good neighbours to have, I thought as I ran up the stairs. (As I found out later, I couldn't have been more wrong.)

I paused outside the glass doors to catch my breath, and then breezed in and gave the front desk manager, one Velu Saar, my most winning smile. After a good half hour, I was ushered into the editor's office.

Mr T.B. Aravindam, or TB as he was popularly known, was a tall, beefy dude. He looked decidedly middle-aged, thirty-five, if he was a day. He was wearing a look-at-it-directly-and-you-will-go-blind bright T-shirt and, wait for it, Ray Ban aviators.

'Rinki, brand new intern! Welcome to *Divaa*!' he said effusively, speaking with this funny just-back-from-the-international-airport accent. 'So, where do we begin?'

Unnerving as it was talking to someone wearing shades indoors, I began by sharing my financial woes. Turned out, his woes were greater than mine.

Like he told me, 'Rinki, I'm sorry to hear you're broke. But we're on a really tight budget. One of our sponsors backed out last month. We're not doing this for money.'

Obviously. Because there wasn't any.

'But we're passionate about what we do. I can see you're passionate about working too.'

And he got that from my resume? Really?

'Don't worry, Rinki. Money will come in life. But what you need right now is experience. Which this internship will certainly provide. As a great man once said, chase excellence and money will follow.'

Hey, didn't Aamir Khan say that in *3 Idiots*? Or was that Chetan Bhagat in *Five Point Someone*?

'We cannot make this a paid internship. But tell you what. If any of your slogans get published in the magazine, we'll pay you for them. One thousand bucks for each.'

A big IF.

'I'll even throw in five hundred bucks for conveyance.'

Wow, how generous. It's what auto guys charge to go down the road.

'So, what do you think, Rinki? You want to give this a shot?'

'I guess so,' I said hesitantly.

'Grrrreat, let's get cracking,' TB said cheerfully, rolling his r's. 'Break a leg!'

I wanted to break his leg. Gosh, I hadn't even started working and I hated my boss already.

I called Robin and Sudha over. For a success party of sorts. We washed down glasses of orange Tang before moving on to the highlight of the day: chilly *bhajjis*. Fried to perfection by Rakamma.

'So, what've you decided, Rinks?' Robin asked.

I told her about the conversation I'd had with TB.

'Hmm, looks like a tough call.'

'What call?' Mom said, gliding out of her room.

'Hello, Aunty!' the girls said in unison, getting to their feet.

'Hello, girls. Sit, sit. I'll join you for snacks.'

'Mom, aren't you going to Malini Aunty's place for early dinner?'

'I am! But nothing beats homemade snacks,' Mom slurped, wolfing down a bhajji. 'Mmmm!'

'Aunty, Rinki was just telling us about her job difficulties,' Sudha spoke up.

I coughed. The last thing I wanted was to discuss my problems with Mom. Nothing good came out of it. Ever. Refer Rinki's *Teen Survival Guide*.

'Job difficulties? But her job hasn't even started,' Mom said, her brows knitted.

'The job will start only if she's able to reach the office, Aunty,' Sudha clucked.

Gawd, I wanted to strangle Sudha.

'What do you mean?'

'Some logistical problems, Mom.'

'You're sounding illogical, Rinki.'

'Transport, Mom. I don't have any,' I said at last, worried that Sudha might move on to my financial difficulties.

'I've been asking her to get a bike for God knows how long,' Mom said theatrically.

'But after the accident, you must be worried, Aunty,' Robin said.

'Accident? What accident?'

'The serious accident she was involved in as a child,' Robin supplied.

'You mean the time her Tobu cycle toppled?'

You know, I always get these things wrong. I should've been more worried about *Mom* spilling the beans.

Two narrowed pairs of eyes turned on me.

'It was a serious accident. I was pinned underneath the cycle!' I asserted.

'Only for a few minutes, Rinki,' Mom said kindly.

A few minutes. That's light years in a child's world! Oh yeah. Mom had certainly taken her time rescuing me.

In a flash, they were back. All those painful memories. The amused expressions on my relatives' faces, the smirk on my idiot cousin's face, the humiliation of it all.

'Er, Mom, I totally forgot! Malini Aunty had called. Asked you not to be late as usual.'

'Oh, I better get going. See you soon, girls! Bye!'

'Bye, Aunty.'

The moment Mom was out of the door, Robin and Sudha pounced on me.

'You were in an accident involving a Tobu cycle?' Sudha asked incredulously.

'I can't believe you were going to turn your job down over a Tobu cycle,' Robin added her two bits.

'Stop saying "Tobu cycle Tobu cycle",' I pleaded, covering my ears with my hands.

'You know what you have to do, right?' Robin said, arching an eyebrow.

'Yeah, I've got to buy the book.'

'Book? What book?' Robin asked, a bewildered look on her face.

'*Learn How to Ride a Bike in Ten days*. It's an international bestseller.'

'Cut the crap, Rinki.'

I stared into the distance miserably. I knew it had to be done. Either that or I'd to kiss my job goodbye. I decided to go with the lesser of the two evils.

Mom and Dad, God bless me, agreed to get me a bike. I didn't have to twist their arms. Too much. Want to know how the conversation went? Remember the hair straightening discussion I had with them? Hit the rewind button and replace the term 'hair straightening' with 'bike'. There you have it.

Plus, it was the more economical option by far. It wasn't merely the question of commuting for the next seven weeks, I had three years of college looming large.

Anyhoo, getting the bike go-ahead was easier than getting my learners' licence. Dad didn't have the time to make a trip to the RTO. Mom didn't have the language skills. Sending me alone was out of the question. So, a fellow Citibank employee was dispatched. Citibank Aunty looked extremely capable, like she could the oil all the wheels of official machinery and oil them well. Cough, cough.

On my part, I had to do severe penance. Spent a whole day in the blazing sun, jumped from one queue to another, clicked an unflattering look-Ma-I-have-orange-jaundice photograph. After testing my patience in every way possible, the traffic gods smiled down at me. I was handsomely rewarded. Rinki 007 finally had the licence to kill, er, cruise.

Fast forward to the next weekend. Rinki Tripathi became the proud owner of gleaming red Scooty. It was a toss-up between that and a lime-yellow Vespa. The Tripathi family voted: red Scooty won.

We even had a small puja for it, courtesy Rakamma. She fixed two lemons beneath the wheels, waved a camphor aarti around it and broke a coconut to ward off the evil eye. I turned the key in the ignition, the wheels went on the lemons, and the riding tutorials were on.

I enlisted everyone's help. And I mean, *everyone's*. I called Google, Robin, Sudha and, on several occasions, even Rakamma. Apparently, I was the only one who didn't know how to ride a bike.

Yes, I made them give me lessons. But trust me, I was doing them all a big favour. Helping them pass the boring summer holidays. Helping them do the good deed of the day. And in Rakamma's case, earning some easy money. I was paying her hundred bucks per class.

It took considerable, time and patience (on the part of the instructors). Many sweaty, gory, teary sessions later, I was good to go. On to the lean mean streets of Chennai.

Watching me practise with such single-minded purpose and determination, even Mom had to remark, 'Good show, Rinki!' Then she went ahead and spoiled it by sighing, 'If only you'd studied for your Board Exams with such dedication.'

Parents. There's no pleasing them.

Anyway, after clocking in what felt like five hundred hours of riding time, and receiving enough 'valuable' tips to last me a lifetime, I was ready.

Valuable Tips:

1. Don't close your eyes when you see a bus speeding towards you. Rakamma. (At least I think that's what she

said. She was speaking too fast. And when it comes to Tamil, I'm kind of s-l-o-w.)

2. Don't go too close to the median. Robin.
3. Don't forget to press the indicator. Robin again.
4. Learn how to ride a bicycle first. Google. (In my defence, I could. Perfectly well, if I may add. Just that I was scared of doing it.)
5. Wear your helmet. Or you will get tanned big time. Self.
6. Always say a silent prayer before you get on the bike. (For the safety of others, I'm guessing.) Mom.
7. With great power comes great responsibility. Dad. (And before him, Spiderman's uncle.)
8. Check your fuel gauge. Don't want you to be stranded on the road. Adit on BBM. (Sweet! But still didn't feel like making up with him.)
9. Maintain your limits. That annoying cop down the road. (He meant 'speed limit', of course.)
10. Keep your eyes on the road at all times. Author of *Learn How to Ride a Bike in Ten Days*.

Movie Genre of the Week: Action

Rinki's Top 10:
1. *Mr and Mrs Smith*
2. *Salt*
3. *Fast and Furious*
4. *Wanted* (Hollywood)
5. *Dhoom*

6. *Dhoom 2*
7. *Agneepath*
8. *Dabangg*
9. *Wanted* (Bollywood)
10. *XXX*

Chapter 10

RinkiTripathi@ChennaiSuperChick
Sign outside concentration camp: Work sets you free.

Warning enough, don't you think?

Oh God, I was so not cut out for a nine-to-five job. Or a desk job. I was so not cut out for a job. Period.

I mean, I always suspected it. And the stint at *Divaa* proved it.

Like most relationships, it started out okay. Guess I was enjoying the first flush of romance. Totally smitten by the boyfriend. In this case, the office, so don't get any funny ideas. All white walls and minimalistic, the only splash of clolour was from from TB's full-sleeved T-shirts.

Velu Saar took me around, introducing me to the fellow sufferers. Everyone wanted to know who I was, where I came from, what I was doing. Gosh, I'd no idea how much I loved listening to the sound of my own voice. (Okay fine, I'd a fair idea.)

I spent the next few days learning, no, not the ropes, the shortest way to the water cooler. Familiarizing myself with the workings of the coffee vending machine. Not to mention, the minds of my co-workers.

There was Loki, the fashion editor. She was a complete sweetheart. I know, I know, her fashion sense was deplorable (she wore sheer black leggings with peep toes, for God's sake). But she was privy to all of Chennai's shopping secrets. Best of all, she didn't mind sharing them. The best stores, the best deals, the best sale previews, she had them all on her fingertips. In fact, I owe half my college wardrobe to her.

The in-house photographer, Suresh, was a darling too. He actually offered to shoot my portfolio. Free of cost! As luck would have it, later that week, TB did a no-show. And you know what happens when the Fat Cat is away. That's right, the mice go astray. Suri and I went straight to the conference room and emerged an hour later with one full-length, two side profile and three close-up shots.

(Quick aside: When I showed them to Mom, she trilled, 'How nice! Keep them safe.' I'd every intention to. But then she spoiled it all by adding, 'When you are twenty-four-twenty-five, we will send this to marriage brokers.' I was so pissed, I almost drew a moustache and beard on all of them. Good thing I remembered they were *my* pictures.)

Velu Saar, the front desk manager, was like the Joan character from *Mad Men*. And about as busty. He was the go-to person for office supplies, leave application forms, conveyance vouchers, hand wash in the loo, and what have you. There was just one problem, he treated office property like his personal property.

Thanks to my doodling habit, I ran out of paper pretty quick and found myself at the receiving end of his lecture.

'One week, one note pad. Like this means, you cut yevery single tree in Chennai,' he said cuttingly. He would have looked less pained had I asked him to part with his daughter's dowry.

'Velu Saar, I'll take one too,' Suri added, waving cheerfully from his desk. 'He's always doing his bit for the environment. Now you know why we call him the Green Man,' he informed me with a conspiratorial wink.

Gosh, really. Velu Saar was always switching off computers (sometimes while we were still working on them), lights and fans. Yevery single time I saw him, he was doing a headcount of pens and pencils.

(Confession: I'm happy to report that I managed to pinch an eraser, a sharpener and a fuchsia pink stapler under Vigilant Velu's eye.)

Coming back to the others members of my extended family. The design team comprised of Anand and Prabhu. Anand was right out of college though he could as easily pass off for a ninth grader. Some people are so lucky. They keep growing old but never once look it.

Prabhu, on the other hand, looked old enough to be everyone's grandfather. But they had one thing in common: they were men of few words. I think their only flaw was that they were over-intimidated by TB.

Like one day, everyone was chilling in the lunch room when TB swept in. Anand leapt up as if a sudden electric charge had gone up his butt and offered his seat to TB. Prabhu didn't know how to make himself useful. So he started sweeping all the bread crumbs that lay scattered on the dining table into his lunch box.

Sigh. It's people like Anand and Prabhu who make tyrants out of bosses.

Anyway, I digress. There were a couple of freelance writers and designers whom I didn't get to meet. They worked from home. Or so they claimed. Ha ha! I heard there were a few marketing managers too. But they were never around, hankering as they were after clients for ads. I bet their official email ids were always in the 'Out of Office' mode.

By far, the MVA, the Most Valued Asset (and inversely, the most underpaid) of the organization was Murali, the office boy. He was forever being sent on some errand or the other, the poor thing.

'Murali, get me lunch.'

'Murali, pick up the parcel.'

'Murali, drop the cheque.'

At least the marketing guys had bikes; Murali had to make do with his cycle. Imagine that in Chennai's all-year-long-sweltering heat.

I felt awful for him. When I shared his plight with Mom, she got to her feet instantly, a steely resolve in her eyes (she was reading the Lead India campaign at the time). She marched across to her wooden almirah, flung the doors open and yanked out a smallish purse. I thought she'd grab a fistful of notes but instead she fished out a key. She unlocked Dad's almirah with a flourish and dug around till she came upon a yellow checked shirt. 'Here, I've never liked this one. Mausiji had gifted it to him,' she said by way of explanation.

Over the next few weeks, Dad's hand-me-downs began to feature regularly in Mom's I-will-make-a-positive-difference-to-Murali's-life plan. Formal shirts, casual tees, trousers, shorts and on one occasion, even his barely-worn kolhapuri chappals. I was only too happy to comply.

I assumed Dad was on board with it. But one fine Saturday, when Murali came home to drop off some old issues of *Divaa*, Dad surveyed him thoughtfully and remarked, 'You know, I have a checked shirt just like that.'

Mom went kind of slow on her charitable endeavours after that.

Much like I did on my professional endeavours. Trust me, it was all going hunky-dory when bam! The electricity crisis hit Chennai. And we were thrown back into the Dark Ages.

Not that I enjoyed shirking work, but it just wasn't humanly possible to think in the absence of electricity. Yeah, all through June (the second hottest month, for crying out loud) the city reeled under the worst power crisis in history. Soon, every area in Chennai was allotted a designated time for power outage. My residential area's was 8-10 a.m., my official area's was 2-4 p.m. Post lunch. Boo hoo! Need I add more?

I challenge anyone to sit through the Chennai heat, bang in the middle of the afternoon, without a fan (guess the powers that be hadn't heard of a generator). Death by furnace, I tell you.

My troubles didn't end there. I was hoping to be assigned a personal computer; instead, I was (grudgingly) handed scribbling pads by Velu Saar. Believe me, I'd no idea how to look busy without a computer. I had to settle for keeping my head bent, drawing little stick figures on unruled note pads.

TB, the editor-in-chief, didn't help matters. He was hardly ever in office. And if by some chance, he happened to be, you wouldn't know it. He was chiefly locked away in his cabin. But when it came to making our lives miserable, he was always there. Shooting down slogans, bombing ideas, ramming his thoughts down our throats. As I figured on the day of my first presentation.

Job at hand: come up with a slogan for *Divaa*.

TB's brief: 'Give me something catchy, give me something catchy.' Sure, TB, would a common cold do?

Deadline: Yesterday.

Total number of options: Thirteen

Top three slogans:

I'm a Divaa. I'm a goddess.
Unleash your inner Divaa.
Divaa. For the Goddess in you.

On the day of the presentation, I even skipped lunch. Didn't want to feel sleepy and all that, you know.

I strolled into the conference room with confidence. Which quickly dissipated the moment I stepped in.

It was so stuffy in there. The windows were sealed shut. The blinds were down. TB's Ray Bans were up though. The power was out. Loki, Suri, Anand, Prabhu were all in. Looking as if they had been forced to attend a public hanging.

That's when I hit the panic button. Dearly beloved, we are all gathered here to mourn the loss of Rinki's enthusiasm.

TB cleared his throat. 'Yes, Rinki, what have you got?'

A severe case of jitters, that's what.

My throat was dry, my palms were clammy. I swallowed hard and rattled off the options, stumbling, stammering, pausing for applause which never came.

When I was done, I sneaked a glance at Suri and Loki. They nodded encouragingly.

I turned my gaze towards Anand and Prabhu. They promptly turned their gaze towards TB.

As usual, TB's expression was inscrutable behind the aviators.

For some reason, he kept tapping his pencil on the table in an unrelenting rhythm. Unbidden, a scene from *The Dark Knight* came floating into my mind. You know, where all the mafia bosses are seated around a table, looking thoroughly displeased, the Joker executes a fellow by slamming his forehead on, what else, a pencil.

'I think the slogans need more work,' piped an unfamiliar voice from the other end of the room.

It was my turn to look as if I was watching *Raaz 3*.

'Oh, sorry! Forgot to introduce myself. I'm Rajesh, head of marketing.'

Oh, that's why he was sorry. Not for making an unsuspecting girl jump out of her skin.

'I'm not sure but something's not right about the slogans,' Rajesh continued.

Why don't you wait till you *are* sure, Rajesh?

I looked at TB.

He looked at the ceiling and kept up that scary thing with the pencil.

'Let's go back to the drawing board. Let's reinvent the wheel. Let's think out of the box,' Rajesh spoke on his behalf.

I was completely crushed. Like a merciless sniper, he had shot all my options down. Bang! Bang! Bang! Each one of them. I hadn't faced so much rejection from boys during my Delhi days.

I pondered over World's Greatest Mystery #34. How do people take all that shit and go back to work the next day?

TB put down his pencil. 'I have an option. For what it's worth, I will share it with you.'

'I'm sure it will be great, TB,' Rajesh said ingratiatingly.

Oh, I'm sure.

'Coming from you, TB, of course, of course,' Prabhu added.

TB got to his feet slowly, like a panther stretching before it went in for the kill.

The air was heavy with expectation. Five faces (excluding mine) watched TB as if he was about to share his Swiss bank account number with them.

'Ah! The joy of being a Divaa.'

There was stunned silence in the room. The big, mighty editor-in-cheap, he'd come up with *that*?

'Oh, TB! Just when I thought you couldn't get any better, you come up with that,' Rajesh said, head bowed in supplication.

'You are thoo good, TB, just thoo good,' Prabhu crowed, drool forming at the corner of his lips.

A giggle escaped me.

Under the table, Loki stamped on my foot. I managed to camouflage the giggle with a full-throated cough in the nick of time.

The discussion dragged on for another hour. I couldn't drag my eyes away from my watch. I'd made movie plans with Google later that evening and I couldn't even tell him I was stuck in a meeting. I didn't have a cell phone, remember?

I called him the second I reached home. As if the whipping I got at work wasn't bad enough, I got an earful from Google. Apparently, he'd waited for an hour outside Satyam Theatre.

At one point, people had started approaching him for tickets, thinking he was a black marketer. When he refused to comply, they pointed him out to a traffic cop. His car was stuck in the parking lot, so he had no choice but to run, the traffic cop hot on his tail. Good thing our cops are out of shape or Googs would have joined Sanju Baba in jail.

I had a crazy dream that night. I was in Spain, running with the bulls, in a pristine white skirt and top. But instead of the bulls goring people with their horns, it was TB. Once he spotted me, there was no stopping him. He let out an enraged roar and ignoring all the red scarves, came thundering down the alley towards me. I woke up in a cold sweat.

Chapter 11

Rinki Tripathi @ChennaiSuperChick
Not all prisons have parole.

Presenting *Alice in Blunderland*

Starring

TB as the Dark Lord

Rajesh as the Loyal Henchman

Velu Saar as the Green Man

Rinki as the Damsel who needs to De-stress

Loki as the Fairy Godmother

Suresh as the Friendly Woodcutter

Murali as the Hard-working Elf

Anand as the Helpless Pawn 1

Prabhu as the Helpless Pawn 2

Guest Appearance—Other marketing managers

Behind the scenes—Freelance writers and designers

Come Monday mornings, I wanted to curl up and *die*. Only I know how I dragged myself out of bed and got ready. To the same old thing all over again. For the life of me, I couldn't fathom how people did it. Day in-day out, five (in some horrifying cases, six) days of the week.

On the other end of the spectrum was my dear Daddy-O. If anything, he suffered from a severe case of weekend phobia. Or maybe I'm wrong. It's entirely possible Mom's mall mania had something to do with it.

Oh I learned quite a bit on the job. But nothing about slogan writing.

And each time I asked TB if I could accompany Loki on her shopping sprees, he'd go: 'Then who will write the slogans?'

You, TB, you.

Top Five Things I learned at Work

1. Boss talks, bullshit walks.
2. Expecting appreciation for hard work is like expecting to wake up in Paris Hilton's body.
3. Meetings will only be called at six o' clock. After you've spent the whole day twiddling your thumbs.
4. Your point of view is like the appendix (the body organ, not the additional stuff at the end of a book): unnecessary.
5. Hoping to strike a work-life balance is like hoping to find treasure buried in your backyard.

Really, work was taking a big toll on my social life. It was those stupid meetings to blame. There were so many of those, and they always began at closing time. And went on and on. By the time I reached home, it was time for the night show, dinner and, of course, my curfew.

Oh, I tried talking my folks into drafting up a new charter: Magna Carta Adulta. But they were acting like the Indian Censor Board, asking for more cuts in the story of my life, denying me the A certificate.

It made me wonder if I'd been too hasty in turning eighteen. I mean, what was the big deal? Sure, it was fun. If you happened to live abroad. Translation, if you could fly the coop, if you could shack up with ACSOTOS (a certain someone of the opposite sex), if you could live on your own terms. But in the prison we call home in Indian society, it was the same old drill. Same ole rules, same ole curfews, same ole negotiations.

I caught up with the wolf pack at The Backyard one weekend and launched into a full-fledged bitchathon. Google cooed, 'Don't worry, Senorita, now nothing will go wrong.'

'Not that dialogue, Googs,' I shuddered. 'Everything goes wrong when Raj says that to Simran in *DDLJ*.'

Hey, did I mention, amongst several other 'qualities', Google also happened to possess a black tongue?

The very next day, we were all huddled in the conference room. For a brainstorming session to discuss the next issue's theme: skin care.

(Quick aside: I love brainstorming sessions. All you need to do is show up. And nod from time to time. If you have something to doodle on, all the better. There's no compulsion to contribute. There's no pressing need to think. Or listen, even. Except to the person before you. And once they are done, you just have to:

A. Paraphrase them

B. Say, 'Exactly my point'

(Plus, there are plates of assorted biscuits going around.)

'So what do you think?' TB asked magnanimously, casting a look around.

Before anyone could so much as open their gobs, he went, 'I think we should interview a dermatologist, throw in some tips, do a double-page spread with Kaya, blah blah.'

'We have to think of a slogan that sums up the issue.'

We? Excusez moi, but I was the only slogan writer around.

TB rambled on. 'I was thinking of "Good skin is the best make up". What do you all think?'

I think it's great, but TB, Lakme already beat you to it.

'Or how about "Let's go skin deep", hmm? Or "The Skintillating Issue?' TB mused aloud.

I was fighting the urge to skin him alive when Mr Velu came barrelling into the conference room.

'Velu! Enna idhu? What is this? What did I say about knocking on the door before coming in?' TB growled.

'C-c-cut, cut, cut,' Mr Velu gasped, moving his index and middle fingers in an ominous gesture.

TB shot out of the room with the alacrity of someone who weighed 50 kgs lesser.

Turned out, the Chennai Corporation guys were paying *Divaa* a long overdue visit. They claimed the entire floor was illegal.

To be sure, they had given the landlord (one Mr Bremanandan) several warnings over the last few months. Asked him to pay the penalty or else. But the Scrooge had chosen to ignore them. In the words of Chennai Corporation, the time had come to teach the bugger a lesson. Bremanandan, in turn, proved that unless a person is willing to learn, you can't teach him shit (pun unintended).

There was nothing we could say or do. TB looked up expectantly at the ceiling. As if an idea would drop from there. Velu Saar did his best to contain the threat, flailing his limbs in a bid to obstruct them. But it was too late.

The corporation croods proceeded to cut off the plumbing with the ruthless determination of a bullet gone astray. Maybe illegal construction is a grievous offence. What I couldn't understand was why our bladders were being penalized for it.

We entreated with TB to talk to the publishing house that owned *Divaa*. He did. The publishers their best to drill sense into that landlord, to make him legalize the construction, to do something and make the torture stop. But I guess in our country 'action' takes place only on the sets of movies.

Hey, the men folk had nothing to lose. I mean, the whole city was their oyster. They could go unleash their pearls anywhere they pleased. Corner of the road, cool. Middle of the street, why not. Walls of the building, absolutely.

Loki was better off. When she was on the move, she was off the hook. So the only person who had to pay a hefty price was ME. In one of my favourite flicks, *The Hangover*, the gang runs around the desert together in Las Vegas, looking for strippers and cocaine. I had to run around far less attractive landscapes scouting for, well, loos.

After being turned away from sundry restaurants, I'd no choice but to 'borrow' loo time from the other offices in the building. Sadly, after the first few days, the bank and the travel agency guys refused to let me in. Complained that I turned up at odd hours, disrupted their schedules. So sorry, my bladder isn't synchronized with yours, guys.

Valuable Lesson Learned in Life: you can never depend on the kindness of strangers. Ultimately, I had to share the ground floor loo with the building watchman. He was none too pleased at the development. Join the club, Uncle.

The worse was having to 'go' in the afternoons. There was no power, hence no elevator. Walking up and down three floors, not easy that. I almost developed Tanni Phobia, the morbid Fear of Drinking Water, you know. People expected me to come up with slogans for a restaurant under such circumstances. All I could think of was 'When you gotta go, you got to goooo'.

Honestly. The experience reminded me of a documentary Dad was once watching on Discovery Channel. On the living conditions of Tihar inmates. Compared to my work environment, theirs seemed luxurious. At least in jail, good behaviour could get you parole or shorten your sentence. At work, you couldn't even hope for that. Once you were in, you were in.

From RT's Secret Diary

My Back-Breaking Work Schedule

10:00 a.m.—Alarm goes off

10:15 a.m.—Hit snooze button on alarm clock

10:30 a.m.—Get out of bed

10:35 a.m.—Jump into the shower

10:40 a.m.——Breakfast: bowl of skimmed milk with honey loops or chocos

10:45 a.m.——Ride to work

11:00 a.m.——Sign in the office register

11: 05 a.m.——Chit-chat with co-workers

12:00 noon——Break for tea/coffee

12:15 p.m.——Depending on comp availability, go online

1:00 p.m.——Break for lunch

1:45 p.m.——Last chance to use elevator, run down to loo

2:00 p.m.——Brainstorm in the conference room

4:00 p.m.——Teatime

4:15 p.m.——Walk down to the loo

4:30 p.m.— Get cracking (crackpot TR's favourite phrase)

6: 00 p.m.——Go in for meeting

7:45 p.m.——Leave for home

7:50 p.m.——Curse traffic

8:00 p.m.——Reach home

8:15 p.m.——Stuff face with mixture and *murukkus*

8:30 p.m.——Vegetate next to Mom while she watches serial, check Blackberry Messenger

8:45 p.m.——Wait for iPad, er, Dad to come home

9:00 p.m.——Go online, update FB status, Tweet

9:30 p.m.——Dinner

10:00 p.m.——Call Robin, Sudha, Google

11:30 p.m.——Watch movie

1:30 a.m.——Turn into Sleeping Beauty

A gruelling routine and a torturous month later, what did I have to show for it? A compromised bladder, that's it.

Movie Genre of the Week: Animation

Rinki's Top Ten:

1. *Ice Age*
2. *Toy Story*
3. *Tangled*
4. *Brave*
5. *Shark Tale*
6. *The Lion King*
7. *The Polar Express*
8. *Madagascar*
9. *Up*
10. *Finding Nemo*

Chapter 12

RinkiTripathi@ChennaiSuperChick
First Day, First Show. For once, I'm not talking about a movie.

You know that uncomfortable feeling you get when you don't belong some place? That no matter how hard you try, you just don't fit in? Well, I used to feel that way at the gym. Now the gym had company. I felt equally ill at ease at college.

I thought I was done with the adjustment crap when I moved to Chennai. But then college happened, and bam! I was back to square one.

Long story short, the Board results came out in May. And while my percentage didn't exactly send Mom and Dad skipping in delighted frenzy, it was actually okay. For someone who didn't exert herself too much.

But when it came to college admissions, exert myself I did. I dutifully accompanied Robin and Sudha to colleges, left, right and centre. Remember my Action Plan? Well, I dropped off my application form at each one of those shortlisted colleges.

Then began the interminable wait. Not for me. For Mom and Dad. I was too busy dying at *Divaa*. Besides, I was sure I would get in *somewhere*. When it came to me, Mom and Dad usually operated from a place of supreme under-confidence.

Turned out, I wasn't the only one with a list system. Chennai colleges have a weird three-list system. Ladies and gentlemen, welcome to the most daunting obstacle race of our lives.

Please put your hands together for the winners. Participants who touch the magical 90-95 per cent score and above. List One.

Sympathetic cluck for the runners-up. The 85-90 per cent and above club. In other words, List Two.

Shake of the head for the so-so club. Those who scraped in with 80-85 per cent. List Three.

Standing ovation for the wait-listed folk. Participants no one wanted. Participants who had to wait for the better lot to find admission elsewhere, leaving a seat open. In certain cases, participants who had to pay their way in. Unofficial List Four.

Perhaps I spoke too soon. Because weeks passed, and my name didn't figure in the first three lists of most colleges. Not WCC, not Ethi, not MOP, not CWC.

Bloody hell! I could only hope for the fourth list. But my parents would never pay to get me in. Not a very hefty amount, in any case.

To make matters more tense, Robin and Sudha figured on CWC's third list. A fact that I had to conceal from Mom and Dad. Couldn't have them going even more ballistic on me.

I was going to get seriously 'katti' with God when Robin called.

'Congo, Rinks! You're on CWC's fourth list!'

Good News: I could start life afresh.

Bad News: Things were going to be no different.

Last week of June, first week in college, we were back to the same old exercise in pointlessness. Introduce yourself, project a good image, say all the right things, get people to like you, form a group with like-minded people. So on and so forth. Gosh, I was so tired. All those people who warned me ('Growing up can be hard') had a point.

So there I was at CWC. Chennai Women's College. At the cost of sounding like their prospectus, it was one of Chennai's premier educational institutions.

Robin and Sudha were in the 'merit' section. I was in the 'at least they will pay the fees' section. God, it was like a modern-day caste system.

Mercifully, we would be together for Hindi class. I would have killed Robin if she'd opted for Tamil or Sanskrit as her second language.

BTW, Google got in to D.D. Vaishnav College, Adit in to Loyola College. No prizes for guessing the list their names figured on.

To make matters more interesting, their newfound bromance was rocking. Two guys cruising around the bylanes of Chennai on a *Sholay* bike? Yeah, that would be them. Back in Delhi, Ankita got into Lady Shri Ram College (info courtesy FB). Not that I was keeping tabs or anything.

Coming back to more important matters. I knew it. I knew on the very first day that I'd made a huge, god-I'm-going-to-regret-this-all-my-life mistake by choosing B.Com. But I'd little choice.

Allow me to explain. See, when it comes to choosing a college, people have different parameters. Criteria 1-100: Academics. Followed by extra-curricular activities.

Well, that's what *regular* folk do. Me? I had my own yardstick:

Rinki's Criteria:

The Crowd: The more cosmopolitan the better.

The (Dress) Code: Chennai was crazy that way. If Delhi college campuses look like fashion show ramps, Chennai colleges don't even look like the backstage area.

The Cool Quotient: The college timings. Couldn't afford to be stuck there for hours on end.

The Company: My wolf pack. How would I survive three years otherwise?

God knows why I had settled for Commerce in XI grade. (Because you sucked at Science and your school didn't have an Arts department, the little voice in my head reminded me. Stupid little voice in the head.)

I had no interest in balance sheets whatsoever. Debit-credit put me to sleep. And the very thought of maths made me break into a cold sweat, even on a scorching summer day in Chennai. But, trust me, the other courses sounded way worse.

Like I kept posting on my Facebook:

BBM. Bachelor of Bank Management—Eeks, the only BBM

I liked was the Black Berry Messenger.

BA Corporate Secretaryship—Yikes, didn't know what that meant and I wanted to keep it that way.

Bachelor of Business Administration—BBA? Bye bye, aye.

BA Economics—Eco was a strict no-no.

BA Literature—Reading books that had sentences beginning with 'Thou art, thou hast'? I'd better run fast!

At the end of the week, Mausiji commented: 'Also, you need higher cut-off marks for all these courses.'

I took a leaf out of the Nike ads. Just did it. Blocked her, once and for all. And Mom too, while I was at it.

I made several important discoveries that first week.

The college was built on a semicircular piece of land. Shaped like the crescent moon. Ringed by a moat, er, a small lane where students basically parked their bikes and cars.

There were several main buildings on campus. Not that I had suddenly taken a keen interest in architecture and all. But there was one that caught my eye. It was right across the lane. The annexe building that housed the Department of Languages. Which meant, students had to go via the back entrance for language classes. Which meant, every day, we would get one shot at freedom.

The back gate was guarded by a couple of very-advanced-in-the-years security personnel. College lore had it that their personal mission was to prevent errant students from bunking. But when has that ever stopped me?

I wasn't quick on my feet. My eyesight couldn't put a hawk to shame. My hearing was no better. But I had a distinct advantage. I had signed up for Hindi. Translation, I could easily pretend to slip into the language building and give them the slip. Ta da!

Oh, one last thing, the canteen served amazingly crisp masala dosas. At ten bucks, they were quite a steal.

And where there is a college, there will be, snore, subjects. They were like my very own Five Pandavas.

Rinki's Five Pandavas

Financial Accounting: Yudhishthir—Very hard to understand, impossible to follow

Business Mathematics: Bheem—The toughest one

Economics: Nakul—Nondescript twin

Business Communication: Sahdev—Same as above

Hindi: Arjun—Easy on the eyes, effortless

The orientation ceremony was just a sign of how dull things were going to be. I thought there would be a party. The seniors would welcome us. There would be music, snacks and drinks (non-alcoholic, of course).

Wrong, wrong, wrong. I was so disoriented by the time the Princy finished reading out from the prospectus. The rules. The regulations. The directions.

Another weird thing about college. In school, everyone knows you. The juniors, the seniors, even the teachers. They know who you are, which batch you belong to, your section, everything. But in college, you're like this invisible being that floats around from one corner to another.

I kind of missed being known for all the wrong reasons. When I told Robin as much, she said it sounded like I was missing school. Ha! Not likely. Or was it?

After two weeks of kill-me-now boredom, I needed a break. I needed to cut class, before they cut off my circulation. Google valiantly agreed to be my accessory in crime. Robin and Suds not so much.

But there were so many things to be taken care of. Where would I leave my bike? If I told Mom I was taking the rick to college, she'd go, 'Then why did you buy the bike?' As if the bike was a Vodafone pug. It *had* to follow me wherever I went.

Anyhoo. I'd every intention of parking my bike in the lane around college. But by the time I reached college, the outside parking was full. Hell! Left with no choice, I parked my Scooty on campus. Then off I went traipsing to Satyam theatre with Googs.

Unfortunately for Google, all shows were houseful except for *What To Expect When You Are Expecting*. I had to wave a caramel popcorn family tub at him to follow me inside the theatre.

After the movie, Google and I made a pit stop for sandwiches at Alsa Mall. It was six by the time we reached college.

The campus wore a deserted look. The security fellows at the main entrance wore fierce expressions. They were standing behind the locked the gates, arms akimbo.

'Oh shoot,' I muttered as I clambered out of the car.

Google was in the process of rolling the glass down and sticking his head out, when *thump!*

'What the hell!' Google bellowed.

One of the security guards had brought his cane down hard on Google's bumper. I mean, his car's bumper.

'Whaat whaat going on?' the security guy demanded.

'Security Saar, my bike! Inside. Ulle ulle.'

Security Saar shot me a look that said he was no ullu.

He fixed me with a scornful look.

'How come you outside, bike inside? Cutting class, aaa?'

'No, no, Saar. After college, crossed road, went ice cream parlour, had butterscotch ice cream.' There was actually a popular ice cream parlour just across the road. Dollops or something.

'Did I ask flavour?' Security Saar Two bared his fangs at me.

'Order took so long to come,' I said meekly.

'Who he?' Security Saar One wanted to know.

Before Google could open his mouth, I answered, 'Anna.' Elder brother.

'Hmmmm. Looks like thambi,' Security Saar said, peering at us. Looks like your younger brother.

Nonsense! In all fairness, I looked at least two years younger to Google. But maybe the stresses and strains of living with such demanding parents had taken its toll. I made a quick mental note: pop a Becosule every day to prevent the aging process.

Security Saars conferred for a few seconds. Much to my relief, they finally let me in. I'd never been happier to see my bike.

Genre of the Week: Chick Flicks

Rinki's Top Ten:
1. *Legally Blonde*
2. *The Princess Diaries*
3. *Bridesmaids*
4. *Sex and the City*
5. *Runaway Bride*
6. *Confessions of a Shopaholic*
7. *The Devil Wears Prada*
8. *Maid in Manhattan*
9. *Made of Honour*
10. *The Ugly Truth*

Chapter 13

Rinki Tripathi@ChennaiSuperChick
You can never outrun your past. Not in Chennai, at least.

Ragging. It's what Sudha was mortally scared of. While it didn't send shivers up and down my spine (I had one, remember), it did bug me no end.

Gawd, I haaaate the very thought of people telling me what to do. Parents, teachers, friends. My funda is simple. I have my own mind, so I'll make my decisions. Thank you very mucking fuch.

So imagine my feelings when the seniors intervened and imposed a dress code for the first one month. No jeans. Salwar kameez only. Oiled hair. Plaits. Flip-flops. And they say Khaap Panchayats are only up North.

I'd no intention of giving in to such ridiculous diktats. I resolutely stuck to my hairstyle. Choosing only to trade my jeans and tees for a frayed salwar kameez. And on one blistery afternoon, paid the bloody price for it.

One minute we were parking our bikes, heading to class and the next, it was Halloween in July. The seniors swooped down on us looking like bloodthirsty vultures.

To our innocent eyes, they looked like Surpanakha, Trijata, Tadaka and all those witches from our epics. There was just one tiny difference. Unlike the fiercely individualistic vamps from the epics, these looked like cast members of *Dracula*.

Dracula's Wife #1, who was at least seven feet tall and about as wide, looked at me as if I were lunch.

Sigh. Gods had divine powers to overcome them. I just had my wits to rely upon.

'What did we tell you kaataans about leaving your hair loose?'

In case you are wondering, 'kaataan' is slang for 'uncivilized'.

'That we shouldn't,' Sudha said, quaking in her Paragon chappals.

All Dracula Wives (DWs) swung around to glare at Suds.

'Speak when you're spoke to, Mini Onion,' spat DW2.

Huh?

'You mean minion, right?' I blurted out.

Uh-oh. Realization dawned. No one likes being corrected. Especially not swaggering seniors in full public view.

Robin looked as if she wanted to tear me limb from limb.

'Oho! Machan, we've a Chinna Shakespeare amongst us,' DW3 crowed.

Chinna = Small.

'Let's take Chinna Shakespeare to the tracks. We'll see how she shoots her mouth off there.'

Not the tracks! Not the frickin' tracks! Anywhere but the tracks.

Legend had it that the most undisciplined of the juniors were taken to the railway crossing. To be ragged alongside boys. Others were let off with a treat or two at the ice cream parlour right outside college. Some were just made to run around the campus. And while I hated any form of physical exercise (not counting making out), I'd have gladly huffed and puffed along the sprawling campus grounds.

No such luck.

'Please, akka,' Sudha pleaded.

'Akka, sorry, akka,' Robin beseeched.

God, where was their self-respect?

Another DW appeared, bakra in tow. A reed-thin girl with a guitar slung around her neck. She was wearing an unfashionably long kurta and faded blue jeans. Retro glasses covered half her face. And her hair, shudder! Remember Preity Zinta's horrible wig from *Lakshya*? Well, that could have been fashioned out of her locks.

'*Paar, machi*! Look what I found, Gangster Rapper!' DW 2 sniggered.

Paar = Look. Machi = female yaar.

Gangster Rapper strummed the guitar loudly in response.

At last, someone had stood up for their rights. Respect.

'I'm a delinquent,' Gangster Rapper said with a touch of pride.

At last, someone with an honest self-image. Respect.

'You know, the music band?'

Oh! She was part of a *band* called Delinquent.

'Back-talk, aa?' DW Two hissed. 'Let's see how much you talk on the way back from the tracks, Jeans Pant.'

We were all shoved into the backseat of a Hyundai Accent and taken to the railway tracks. Robin prayed all the way. Sudha exhausted a lifetime's supply of tears. Gangster Rapper merely plucked at her guitar strings. I just gaped at her.

Presently, the tracks came into view. So did a bunch of boys. The ones marching were the juniors, no doubt. The ones going 'Left, Right, Left,' were the seniors.

My heart was hammering inside my chest. So, it was no urban legend. We were going to be ragged with male fellow freshers. Damn!

'Okay,' DW1 barked. 'Now there's a task for each one of you . . .'

'Didn't know I was on *Roadies*,' I muttered. Robin shoved her elbow into my stomach.

'What did you say?' DW2 hissed, cocking an ear. 'Acting like a qyoon, aa?'

Qyoon? What the hell was that? DW2 drew an imaginary crown on her head. Sigh. She meant queen.

'Forward march,' DW3 bellowed.

I did.

'Take an imaginary rose in your hand and go propose to all the boys there.'

Under ordinary circumstances, this would have been any girl's dream. Proposing to every guy under the sun without fear of judgement. But not me. I don't even shop that way. I have got to like an outfit before I even consider it. Oh yeah.

But a shove from the witches sent me flying.

There was a long queue of scared-looking guys, their hair as oily as Sudhey's.

They hadn't been allowed to wear jeans either. Most were wearing baggy trousers and Govinda-bright shirts. And rubber chappals. Poor things.

I started the ritual. I went up to the first guy in the queue and gestured at him to extend his palm.

'Sorry, sister, I can't,' the first recipient said, tears welling up in his eyes.

Oh, for God's sake. It wasn't as if I was robbing him of his virginity.

Angrily, I thrust the imaginary flower into this hand. 'Lau you,' I mumbled.

In my head, saying 'lau' didn't seem to be such a betrayal to the future guy of my dreams.

I must have finished fifteen proposals when I got near their seniors. About a dozen of them were lounging in various poses against the car.

'What, no rose for me?' A dizzyingly familiar voice breathed in my ear.

I FROZE. Correction, I DIED.

It COULD NOT be. It just couldn't.

The lust of my life. My once-upon-a-time boyfriend. Definitely-maybe-oh-I-don't-know boyfriend. The hottie who drove me batty. It couldn't be. But it was. It was him. Tejas. My very own McDreamy.

No, no, no.

Not when I was wearing a hundred-year-old salwar kameez. Not when rivers of sweat were running down my face. Not when my hair was messier than my wardrobe. Gawd, could I BE more unlucky?

And then it struck me. Lady Luck hadn't completely deserted me. I'd defied the hair-in-two-oily-plaits diktat. I would have died if Tejas had seen me like that. Never to be reborn. Breaking the cycle of birth and rebirth, despite the mountain of bad karma I'd accumulated over the years.

I didn't dare breathe. I didn't dare move.

'Rinki?' He tapped me on the shoulder. That touch! I jumped as if he had poured a tray full of ice cubes down my back.

In one swift motion, I whipped around and was face to face with the guy of my dreams.

Gosh, he looked dishier than before. If that was possible. His face looked more angular. His hair looked spikier. His arms were beefier. And his chest! The very sight of it made me want to hurl myself at it. He seemed to have shot up by another two inches. Or maybe it was because I wasn't wearing heels. Oh crap. His yummy thin lips were stretched into his trademark smirk. His blazing brown eyes were digging right into my soul.

You know that song from *Delhi Belly*, 'I hate you like I love you'? It started playing in loop in my head.

'Well, well, well. If it isn't Miss Tripthi,' he drawled, referring to me by the irritating nickname that had stuck in school. It usually oscillated between Tripthi, Tirupathi and Tri-patty.

I stood there like one of those statues on Marina Beach.

'You haven't changed,' Tejas continued, appraising me coolly.

How the hell was I supposed to translate that sentence?

You're still the Amma you always were.

I was hoping to see an improvement.

You look cool as ever.

I was so bugged. It'd been, what, one year? How much could one possibly change in one year? Then I thought of all those people who go through plastic surgery, liposuction and makeovers. Why, oh, why couldn't I be those people? I should have done all those things. That would have served him right. Made him eat his heart out. Made him realize what he had lost out on.

'Your hair's different.'

Aha!

'It used to have a mind of its own,' Tejas continued, his voice dangerously soft.

What else did he remember? My heart started beating at the speed of light.

An uncomfortable silence ensued.

'So, Tirupathi, what brings you here?' TJ said at last.

'Oh, I came for my afternoon jog, what else?' I said sweetly.

That drew a chuckle out of him. 'Ah, the famous Tripathi Repartee! Always the firebrand, my li'l Rinki.'

I. Was. Not. His. Li'l. Rinki.

So was not.

I was about to swoon but the sharks came swimming up to us.

'Hey! Why you interrupting Chinna Shakespeare?' DW2 pouted.

'Is that what they're calling you these days?' TJ wanted to know.

I ignored him.

'I've finished proposing to all the guys,' I informed DW2. I cast a glance over my shoulder. Poor Robin and Sudha were going through the same motions.

Tejas tossed a devilish look in my direction. 'Really? She hasn't proposed to me.'

Swine!

'Good idea. Let's make the juniors propose to all the seniors now,' said DW3. Sniffing blood, she had come slithering up to us.

'Well, actually, I just meant me,' Tejas drawled in that maddening tone of his.

He gave me a look that, hand-on-heart, made my toes curl. Gosh, I wanted to hail a passing auto and jump into it, no negotiation nothing.

'Tripthi,' he said abruptly. 'Why don't I drop you home?'

Beg your bloody pardon? I couldn't possibly be in the same car with him. Memories of the time we'd spent in his car came rushing back. Making me blush furiously.

The corners of TJ's mouth contorted. He knew what I was thinking.

I suddenly had a vision of me clinging to the salwar bottom of DW2, wailing, 'Nooooo, don't let him take me away, akka!'

'Tirupathi, I'm sure you've had enough of getting to know your seniors?'

Oh, that's what it was? A getting to know session. In civilized parts of the world, we do it over a nice meal.

'Thanks, TJ, but no thanks. I'd rather stay here.'

'Why, Rinks? What's going on in that head of yours?'

Oh, nothing much, TJ. Let me see. Only a few pressing questions.

Why did you break off with me?

Why the hell did you ride off into the sunset with that bimbo Priya?

Why didn't you ever keep in touch?

Why didn't you Facebook me?

Take off your shirt, TJ, and tell me the truth

'Nothing,' I said out loud. 'I-I-I can't abandon my friends.'

'I'd be happy to drop them as well.'

I knew he would. It wouldn't be the first time.

But there was another hitch. Robin hadn't really approved of Tejas. Always maintained that he was all wrong for me. She was right, of course. But back in the day, I'd countered it with, 'How could something so wrong feel so right?'

Anyway, it was all in the past. Water under the bridge and stuff.

'Aww, don't crash our party, Tejas,' pouted DW1.

'Don't you have other lambs to pick on, ladies?' Tejas asked them coolly.

The DWs shot us a venomous look which simultaneously translated to:

We aren't done yet.

You can run but you can't hide, suckers.

Tejas may have saved you today but your ass is ours.

'Go, get your friends, Tri-patty,' Tejas ordered.

I ran.

I must confess, for the first time in her life, Robin looked happy to see Tejas.

Sudha looked as if she wanted to do a shashtang namaskaar

for him. You know, the traditional, flat-on-the-ground, feet-touching gesture.

We clambered in to TJ's gleaming white Swift Dzire. I didn't speak a word during the drive. Oh, Tejas tried. But none of us were in the mood. Presently, he pulled up at my place.

'Tell me you've got a cell phone now, Rinki.'

Sudha let out a pitying sigh.

Tejas groaned.

'Same landline?'

Yeah, feel free to call like you didn't last time.

'Thank you so much, Tejas. Really appreciate it,' Robin said, clambering out.

'Anytime, girls. I don't bite, you know,' he said with a wink.

'I'm sure you don't,' Sudha said loyally.

I nodded frostily as I let myself out, slamming the door shut on him.

As I soon realized, slamming the door on your past is not quite that simple.

The moment we stepped in, my landline rang.

'Must be Loverboy calling,' Robin said wryly.

I dropped my bag on the floor and marched purposefully towards the phone. 'Don't be silly, Robin. Hello? Oh hi, TJ! Wasn't expecting to hear from you. Umm, yeah, uh, okay. Fine, bye.'

I hung up, my heart pounding.

'Let me guess, Loverboy's asked you out,' Robin guessed accurately.

'Stop calling him that! And yes, he did.'

'So where is it this time? Satyam theatre? Barista? Amethyst?' Robin asked, mentioning all the old hotspots that had played a prominent role in the Rinki-TJ love story, version one.

'His place, actually,' I admitted sheepishly.

'Wow, he doesn't believe in wasting time.'

'Robin, pleasssseeee, stop being so weird. He called me *home*, where parents live, you know? No scope for any hanky-panky there.'

'Or maybe the parents will be conveniently out of town,' Robin said, arching an eyebrow.

'Yes, like how Sriram called you over when his parents had gone on a pilgrimage to Madurai,' Sudha added innocently.

'Sudha!' Robin cried out, looking daggers at her.

'Thanks, Suds,' I added wryly.

'Hardly the same thing!' Robin cried out. 'We are truly, legitimately, honourably going out.'

'Well, so could Rinki and Tejas,' Sudha said a bit timidly.

'No chance of that happening, girls,' I assured them.

'Then why's he calling you over?' Robin wanted to know.

'I don't know. Maybe he wants to say something, clear things out, give an explanation.'

'And what do you want, Rinks?'

True love. Pots of money. Peace of mind.

I shrugged. 'I've no intention of meeting him. Not now, not ever.'

'Good idea, Rinks,' Robin plopped down on the couch with a sigh. 'He's already broken your heart once.'

'Not really,' I said bravely.

Yes, really. Biiiiiig time. He'd crushed my love-struck heart underfoot when he dropped out of my life. No explanation, nothing. It was like those sad movies where the hero just walks on and never looks back at the camera. Only thing, in this case, the camera happened to be *me*.

Sure, I could have called him, demanded an answer. But then I'm not one of those things you spread outside the door, you know. I had my pride.

As it were, getting over him had been such a task. It'd taken tremendous powers of self-control (that I didn't know I possessed). I'd cried my eyes out for weeks. I'd thought about him every second, every minute. I'd played and replayed every conversation in my head. Oh, it was AWFUL.

Everything had reminded me of him. Places, songs, things. But then one day, I read about how Kristen had cheated on Robert, and I'd felt instantly better. I mean, if it could happen to *him*, what chance did a lesser mortal like me have?

And now when I'd finally moved on, he was back. Flashing those annoyingly gorgeous baby browns at me.

I'd a lot of thinking to do. Precisely what I did the second Robin and Sudha left.

Asked myself a few hard-hitting questions (In fact I'd recommend these to all the pining youth out there):

1. Don't you want to be with someone who wants to be with you?
2. Don't you deserve to be happy?
3. Don't you think you can do better than your current flame?

If like me, you answered all the above questions in the negative, you'll be fine. Oh, not right away. That would be a little too much, no. But eventually, you'll be fine. Trust me.

The day of the date, I was so jittery. I felt as if I was starring in this big budget movie called *Unfinished Business*. Starring Rinki Tripathi and Tejas Ramchandran. Supporting Roles: Dracula's Wives. Negative Role: Priya the Vamp. Guest Appearance: Robin and Sudha.

For all the big talk, my confidence level was close to zero, wait, make that minus. I just didn't know what to wear. Sure, it was a PPO (Purely Platonic Outing), it certainly didn't qualify for a date. But still. Dressing for the day is so much more challenging, you know. At night, you can pour yourself into something black and voila! All your flaws are taken care of. But in broad daylight, every jiggly bit is out there for all to see.

There would be no second chances. I had to get it right. I donned my thinking beret.

I pulled out everything from my closet, placed it on the bed. Each and every top, each and every accessory. Right then, Mom happened to walk in. One look at the heap on the bed, and she looked distinctly impressed.

Quick aside: The last time she'd walked in on me getting ready for a date, I'd passed the exercise off as a 'wardrobe audit'. So she couldn't help but marvel at yet another cleanliness drive. 'Carry on, Rinki!'

I did as I was told.

The outfit had to be just right. Nothing too revealing. Nothing too boring. Something casual, something effortlessly chic. I didn't want to look as if I was TTH. Trying too hard, you know. Finally, I opted for a floral print dress. I teamed it up with a broad brown belt and matching Aldo wedges. An oversized pair of Mango shades completed my look.

I think TJ approved. Because the minute I clambered into the passenger seat, his face broke into an ultra-pleased smile.

'Tripthi,' he said warmly. 'You look sweet.'

'I aim to please,' I said coolly. But of course, I was super thrilled! I bet even coming All India First in the Boards wouldn't have felt this good. I look sweet, I look sweet, my heart sang.

'Will remind you the next time you're arguing your head off.'

'I don't argue my head off,' I said heatedly. For the next ten minutes, I did exactly that.

Hey, it was the first time I was visiting his place. I was feeling kind of jumpy. I'm not exactly sure about the protocol for ex-couples. But surely, a coffee shop would have been a better option?

'Gorgeous,' I commented.

'You mean me or the apartment?'

Excuse me! That sounded suspiciously like, you know, F-L-I-R-T-I-N-G. Or was I acting like one of those silly girls? Mistaking mere banter for flirtation?

Tejas lived on the twelfth floor of a high-rise on College Road. And the view was as beautiful as him, if not better.

'Make yourself at home, Trips.'

'Where are you parents?' I asked, looking around.

'Parent,' he corrected. 'My folks split up.'

Oh. My. God.

'Been over a year now.'

No wonder he seemed so distracted back in school. He had some serious stuff to deal with at home.

It was all coming together only now, like the climax of a Quentin Tarantino movie. TJ was damaged goods. I bet he had all those issues—Daddy, trust, commitment.

'Didn't you know?' TJ asked softly.

My jaw was on the floor. Is that the expression of someone who knows?

'I live with my mum.'

'Where's she now?'

'In Bangalore.'

'Bengaluru,' I corrected him. Gosh, I could have kicked myself.

'Visiting my elder brother. I didn't know you wanted to meet her,' he said teasingly.

'I didn't,' I protested. 'I mean, I would have loved to . . . I mean, I wouldn't mind . . .' What was wrong with me?

TJ grinned impishly.

I opened my mouth to retort but he ambled over to the music system. He jabbed at a button and Enrique's 'Tonight I'm loving you' came on.

WTF! I thought this was a purely platonic meeting. This once, I wasn't reading too much into things.

Ting tong! Ting tong!

No, no, those weren't alarm bells going off in my head. Just the doorbell.

Tejas got to feet and an instant chatter filled the room. A gaggle of girls barged in, all pausing to hug and smack the air near Tejas' ear.

What was this, Tejas ka Swayamvar?

'And who's this?' cooed one of the trolls.

'Yes, TJ, introduce us to your little friend,' trilled another fugly babe.

TJ? TJ! That was my name for Tejas. Troll!

'Pratyusha, Shaina, Shruthi, meet Rinki. My junior from school.'

Oh, so that's what I was. A junior? Niiiiice!

'You always had the hots for younger girls,' Pratyusha said, punching him in the arm.

Tejas gave her a playful shove. 'Where are the guys?'

'Oh, you know how punctual our boyfriends are!' Pratyusha said with a merry laugh.

Did someone say boyfriends? Suddenly, the girls didn't seem so bad. One was, I think, wearing a rather nice FCUK top.

'They're never on time.'

'Chill, Tejas, they are on the way. Went home to change after the match,' Shaina answered.

The doorbell rang again. Pratyusha and Shaina raced up to their BFs, Deepak and Arun. Soon, TJ's living room was flooded with people.

Here I'd been thinking TJ had called me over to have his wicked way with me. I was soooo sooooo stooopid.

I craned my neck to see but TJ seemed to have disappeared.

Someone changed the CD.

Suddenly, he was by my side. With two long-stemmed glasses of wine.

Unthinking, I accepted them both.

His mouth twisted as if he was about to say something. But then he just shrugged and disappeared into the crowd again.

Over the next half an hour, I got busy draining the glasses.

'So, Rinks, what have you been up to all these days?' TJ murmured in my ear.

Damn! You ought to stop doing that, TJ.

'Oh, this and that,' I said, a trifle dismissively.

'I want to know everything,' Tejas ordered as he refilled my glasses.

'Why?'

Sure, he had problems at home. But the way he'd cut me off! And now, he was acting like I was a best friend who'd just returned from Iraq.

'What do you mean why, Rinks? I just want to know.'

'Why now? Where were you all these months? What makes you think you can come barging into my life again? What makes you think you can just pick up where you left off?'

It was the wine talking. Definitely the wine talking.

Alcohol in wine: 13 per cent

Dutch courage in wine: 100 per cent

I mean, I could never ever say a rude word to someone who looked like *that* under normal circumstances.

'I was wondering when all that pent-up rage would come out.'

'You're making me sound like the Hulk.'

'Go, Hulk! Get everything out of your system. Say everything you've bottled up for so long.'

So I did exactly that. True to his word, not a peep came out of his mouth. When I was done with all the recriminations and accusations, he whistled.

'That's quite a list. That's it?'

'For the time being,' I said crossly.

'May I present my case, Your Honour?'

I wanted to hit him with a gavel and say, 'Proceed.'

'Triparty, you're sweet and saucy.'

Great, now I sounded like ketchup.

'You're fun-loving and funny.'

Yeah, that's what hot guys look for in chicks.

'You're stubborn and opinionated. Impulsive and irreverent.'

He paused for effect. What, I was supposed to give him a standing ovation for tabulating all my weaknesses?

'But you really are something.'

Oh, keep going, don't stop now.

'I know I acted like a complete . . .'

'Ass,' I supplied.

'I was going to say "moron" but that sounds appropriate too,' Tejas conceded. 'But you were always so aloof, so distant . . .'

Aloof? Distant? Me? I'd practically thrown myself at the guy at every given opportunity.

'I thought you didn't care . . .'

Exact opposite, *exact* opposite!

'At times, I felt you weren't that into me . . .'

On those rare occasions, I was trying to play it cool. Dumb bloody idea.

'And then things got so bad at home . . .'

Just my luck.

'So I thought it was best to leave things at that.'

Best to leave me, more like.

'What I'm proposing, Miss Rinks, is this.'

Proposing? Interesting choice of words, Mr T. I leaned forward and almost ended up falling off the couch. His hands shot out to grab my shoulders.

Every fibre of my being started tingling.

Out of nowhere, Shruthi the tart appeared and started pulling TJ to the makeshift dance floor. Where several loose-limbed chicks were dancing.

'Dance with us, Tejas,' she shrieked, shaking her bounteous bottom.

TJ extricated himself from her paws as gently as he could and shooed her away.

'So what was I saying, Rinks?'

'You were proposing . . . hic.'

TJ's eyes crinkled.

'Yeah, I was.'

My heart flipped over in my chest.

'Pure friendship. No strings attached.'

And that made me think of the movie that went by the same name. Where the hero and heroine intend to be friends, only to end up making booty calls to each other. So, we could be 'F' Buddies? And I don't mean Facebook buddies, for God's sake. Is that what he had in mind?

'Nope, not that,' Tejas answered my unspoken question.

Good looks. Hot bod. And now he could read my mind. Hoo boy, I was in trrrrouble.

'I just want to get to know you better first.'

First! And once he got to know me?

'I screwed up the first time around,' TJ continued, reaching for my hands. 'I'd really like to make up for that.'

'What about Priya?' I countered.

'What about her?'

'Won't she mind?'

TJ raised his eyebrows. 'Why will she? From what I hear, she's happily dating two guys.'

Just like me, not so long ago. Of course, Tejas needn't know that.

'So you and Priya?'

'A closed chapter since Class 11.'

Hmmm. Guess it was time to stop digging into his X-Box, if you know what I mean.

'Surely you know that, Rinks?'

How the hell would I know that? Had he ever bothered to clear the air? Ever cared to spell things out?

'So, friends?' he asked solemnly, proffering a hand.

I hesitated.

'Unless you want to be something more than that?' Tejas asked, his eyes gleaming.

That was it. The final straw. The comment that drove me to the edge.

'Are you crazy? Am happily dating two guys meself, hic.'

Shoooooot! I did not mean to let THAT out.

He sank back into the couch, an unreadable expression on his face.

'Really?' he said at last. 'I wouldn't have pegged you as the kind.'

'Like you said, you hardly know me,' I said evenly.

'True,' he mused, tossing me another intense look. 'Going to be interesting, getting to know you, Rinks,' Tejas finished the sentence ominously.

Under that gaze, I thought I'd self-destruct. You know, like the phoenix in those *Harry Potter* movies.

Back home, I wanted to kick myself for spilling the beans about Adit and Google. It wasn't even true. Anymore. Adit was Ankita's flavour of the season. And the only woman in Google's life was his gym instructor. And she was wayyy more manly than our Googly.

I wish I could have discussed the new developments in my life with Ankita. But, as I reminded myself, she was the Public Frenemy Number One.

I didn't hear from TJ for the next few days. Which, by the way, passed in a blur. I settled down in college. Painfully adapted to the 12:30 to 5:30 routine. I just had to cultivate the right attitude towards it. That's all. So I did exactly that. I went to college the way I went for a Bollywood potboiler. Left my brains back at home.

To my surprise, Gangster Rapper turned out to be my classmate. My benchmate, to be more precise. Like most people, she even had a real name. Kadambari.

Classes were held in a big gallery with steps. No one was willing to sit in the last row. Except her and yours truly. While we did not chat much, we sat in companionable silence. Well, kind of. Most days, she simply plugged in her earphones and dropped dead on the desk. I would have loved to catch up on my sleep as well. But someone had to give proxy for her.

I missed having Robin and Sudha in my section. But we more than made up during the Hindi period. We'd clamber up, pounce on the last row, open our textbooks and yak away to glory. That was the best sixty minutes of my day.

Too bad, our Hindi teacher, Mrinalini Ma'am, sniffed it out soon enough. So the minute she'd walk into class, she'd go, 'You last row girls. Yes, you, Rinki, Robin, Sudha. Go sit in three different corners of the class.'

Just like that, it felt like we were back in school.

Movie Genre of the Week: Musicals

Rinki's Top Ten:

1. *My Fair Lady*
2. *The Sound of Music*
3. *Chicago*
4. *High School Musical*
5. *Step Up*
6. *Hum Aapke Hain Kaun*
7. *Hum Dil De Chuke Sanam*
8. *Mary Poppins*
9. *Grease*
10. *Mamma Mia*

Rinki Tripathi is taking an online quiz on Teenz Forever

Quiz # 877: Can you be friends with your ex?

1. Describe your break up in one word:
   a. Beep! Beep! Bitter
   b. Oh, it was civil. Didn't delete him from FB or anything
   c. Don't quite remember
2. Back in the day, you were described as:
   a. The can't-keep-their-hands-off-each other-couple
   b. Good friends
   c. Yawn, next question

3. Who used to be the first one to make up after a fight:
   a. The person who made the mistake: him
   b. We took turns
   c. How does it even matter?

4. Were you the dumper or the dumpee:
   a. Ha ha, what a joke. Dumper, of course
   b. It was a mutual decision
   c. Couldn't care less

5. The first time you saw your ex with their new flame, you:
   a. Wanted to slap their stupid smiling faces
   b. Went up and congratulated them
   c. Are we done here already?

Can we slap you right now? Good lord! It doesn't matter what you've scored. To hell with the ABCs. Do not get back with the ex. Not for a minute. Not for a second. Not at all. No, nyet, nahi, nope, ille, nakko. How many lingos do you want to hear that in? You can set the prophecy in stone: you will live to regret the day. There's a reason why you guys broke up in the first place. Chances are, all those reasons still exist. So do yourself a favour, okay? Axe the ex. Like now! Getting back, in any form, is a bad, bad idea. Nothing ever came out of befriending an ex. Just ask Robert Pattinson.

Chapter 14

RinkiTripathi@ChennaiSuperChick
100 per cent mischief. 0 per cent regret.

I'd discovered during my days of employment that it was against my basic grain to sit still. Expecting me to do so five hours in a row, five days a week was expecting a bit much. I was always on the lookout for excuses to bunk.

Moreover, college had so many rivals competing for my attention. Mum's cell phone, social media networking, friends, cinema halls, coffee shops, discotheques . . . Over the next three months, I divided my time fairly between all the above suitors. But then something happened, something unexpected which tilted the scales in the favour of one.

All through August, my routine was fixed. Well, kind of.

Saturdays—they were the best days of the week. Rinki's-Day-Out-with-TJ days of the week. Like those hard-core dieters, who'd kept temptation at bay, I felt I deserved a weekend treat. And TJ with his taut abs and tight tees was just what the dietician ordered. Slurp! We hung out at his place. Surrounded by his friends, their girlfriends, and, sigh, his gaming console.

As for Sundays, they were spent hibernating at home.

Mondays were Gallivanting with Google days. Both of us suffered from Mon-morn phobia, the fear of Monday mornings. We could handle things much better in the cool environs of a mall or cinema hall.

I tried devoting Tuesdays to Morrie, er, Mommy. Did my best to convince her that once a week a la Kit Kat, break toh banta hai. She wouldn't hear of it. Not even when I promised to ferry her around on the bike. But she was quick to take me up on my offer on Saturdays. Temples, tailors, departmental stores, Nallis, there wasn't a place she spared. But college it was on Tuesdays.

So Tuesdays, Wednesdays and Thursdays were spent doing jail time. I'd exhausted all my options. Nowhere to go, nothing to do. So college it was.

Fridays were spent cutting class with Robin, Sudha and a bunch of girls from their section. In their heart of hearts, they felt less guilty doing so on the last day of the week. Talk about being dil-logical.

Soon, I was better acquainted with girls from the other section than with my own classmates. I'd no clue what most of them looked like. If I bumped into them on the street, I wouldn't be able to recognize them. I could barely tell the teachers apart, for crying out loud.

Let me see. Mrinalini Ma'am was the one who taught Hindi. Ragini Ma'am taught Economics. The one who dressed shabbily and dragged her feet was Geetha Ma'am. She taught Financial Accounting. I think.

The one who never waxed her arms and upper lip was our Business Maths teacher, Bindu Ma'am. Alas, she was also the Head of the Department. The moment she entered class, fun came to a big round bindu (full stop).

We couldn't get a moment's respite with her around. She was one of the rare breed of teachers who'd walk up the entire steps and check on us.

She had a healthy mistrust of backbenchers and delighted in hauling us up from time to time. She'd no clue about our names, of course. She'd just point a thick finger at me and address me by the clothes I was wearing on the day.

If I happened to be in a leopard print top, she'd go, 'You Singham, solve the problem. Come down and work it out on the blackboard.' If it was a floral top I'd gone with, she'd be like, 'Quick, answer the question, Poo.' Before you wrinkle your nose in disgust 'Poo' means flower in Tamil. If Kadambari was in bunk mode, she'd clamour, 'What happened to your best friend? Haven't seen her at all.'

In the beginning, I was quick to point out that Kaddy was not my best friend. But my protests fell on deaf ears. Soon, everyone, teachers and students alike, started referring to her as my best friend. After a while, I just gave up.

So if anyone asked me for her whereabouts, I'd say the first thing that popped to my mind. 'She'd to take her dog to the vet', 'She fell down the stairs and hurt her shin', 'They have a show coming up, she's got band practice today'.

In the end, I proved to be a loyal friend, after all. Because I religiously gave proxy for her, Kaddy performed exceedingly well in one sphere. Attendance.

Kaddy herself was untouched by all the college madness. She was like those virginal Hindi film heroines. The ones who were sold into the flesh trade, yet managed to stay lily pure even as nasty business went on all around them.

As Bindu Ma'am read out from the Scroll of Shame, at the end of the first term, 'Rinki Tripathi 65 per cent attendance, Kadambari Ramesh 70 per cent'. I still don't know how hers turned out to be better than mine.

Bindu Ma'am informed us that we needed to have at least 75 per cent to sit for half-yearly exams. First-time offenders were let off with a stern warning ('Keep this up and your parents will be summoned! In the worst case scenario, no hall ticket will be issued!')

It was enough to keep me off the roads for a while. Until the end of the exams, in any case.

Seventy-five per cent. Anyone catch the irony here? Our attendance had to be better than our marks. That's why I worry about the future of our country.

Anyhoo, thanks to Robin's expert coaching, I hit the magic mark across all the subjects with relative ease.

Convincing Mom to call off the Saturday bike expeditions proved far tougher. Ultimately, fate had to intervene.

Here's what happened. Helmets securely in place, Mom and I were on the way to T. Nagar for window shopping. I'd just turned into a one-way, when a mini bus came bearing down at us. From the wrong side of the road! I panicked and swerved the bike to the left. Only to end up losing my balance.

Thuddd!

Mom and I crashed on the ground unceremoniously. Mom leapt to her feet with an agility that took me by surprise. 'How daaaaaaare he! Get up, Rinki, get up! Don't let him get away!'

With Mom's hysterical cries of 'Follow him, follow himmmmm' ringing in my ears, I kick-started the bike, spun it around and revved the accelerator. I shot down the road, overtook the bugger in true Bollywood style, praying he'd have the good sense (and the reflexes) to brake in time.

Screeeeeeeeeech!!!

Remember the invigorating aarti (cymbals, bugles, drumbeats and all) from Sanjay Dutt's movie *Vaastav*? It started playing in my head. At full volume. Mom got down from the bike in one swift motion.

She galloped to the mini bus and banged her furious fists on the driver's side of the door.

'Saale, nikal bahar!'

As they say, you can take someone out of Delhi but you can't take Delhi out of them.

I parked the bike on the side of the road and hurried to her side.

'Mom, let's not get carried away, please. No point creating a scene and all.'

The driver jumped down. He gingerly inspected his side of the door for damages. The gall!

'Enna rascalla?' Mom unleashed her full fury at him.

'Madam, decency maintain, pliz.'

'You maintained decency, haan? Speeding, hitting, running. Got any sense? Nonsense!'

The driver held up his hands. 'By mistik, okay. Me not knowingly do eet.'

'Khaaamoshhhhh!' Mom thundered, sounding like a fearsome female Shotgun Sinha.

Seeing as Mom was in no mood to back down, the driver adopted a reconciliatory approach. 'Whaaaat Ma, why you are shouting so much?' he said in mollifying tones.

Mom's decibels went notches higher. 'SAY SORRY! NOW! Or your Ma won't be able to recognize you!'

By this time, a curious crowd of onlookers had started to gather around us.

'SAY SORRRRRRRRYYY!'

The driver appeared to consider Mom's 'request'. But one look at her Bhadrakali avataar and he folded quicker than the Indian cricket team's middle batting order. 'Sarry, sarry, sarry,' he chanted, crossing his arms to touch his ears in a never-again gesture. I half expected him to fall at Mom's feet.

Come evening, Dad was debriefed about the event. He promptly suggested Mom take the car and company driver on Saturdays. If he could have his way, he'd have sent the driver on Sundays too.

And that's how, I was taken off duty. Yay!

Genre of the Week: Comedy

Rinki's Top 10:
1. *Me, Myself & Irene*
2. *Meet the Parents*
3. *The Hangover*
4. *Golmaal 3*
5. *Bol Bachchan*
6. *There's Something about Mary*
7. *The Mask*
8. *Andaz Apna Apna*
9. *American Pie*
10. *Delhi Belly*

Chapter 15

RinkiTripathi@ChennaiSuperChick
Hello, Pumpkin, pumpkin! Hello honey bunny!
Feeling something something, hello honey bunny!

I'd sworn I'd ease up on my bunking routine. As it happened, I did the exact opposite.

Come September, the Tejas Tsunami struck my life big time. In the face of all that gorgeousness, all my good intentions flew right out of the window. Taking my old routine along with them.

Soon, it became harder and harder to keep track of the days. I'd no clue when the week began and when it merged into the weekend.

Yeah, Rinki T and TJ had gone from just friends to good friends. In the Bollywood sense of the term. How did that happen? Let's take it from the top, shall we?

Things were hunky-dory. It was all going as per the friends-without-benefits plan. TJ and I were meeting (as opposed to 'seeing') each other regularly. So much so that I was convinced, it *was* possible to be friends with your ex.

148

We were hanging out at Eco Cafe or Amethyst. Places my friends weren't likely to frequent (they were loyal patrons of Café Coffee Day and Barista). To be sure, it was only coffee. The ads have it all wrong, you know. Nothing ever happens over coffee.

Or over lunch outings, for that matter. Notice the emphasis over the word 'outings'. That's because we went dutch. TJ insisted on paying, of course. But this time around, I didn't want to send the wrong signals. It blew a hole in my modest savings but some things had to be done.

That's how things stood for a while. And then came the matinee.

Take it from me, if you want to stay friends with ACSOTOS (A Certain Someone Of The Opposite Sex), do NOT go for a movie.

Even if it happened to be a hardcore action movie. That's because the real action would unfold *off* the screen. You could start off throwing popcorn at each other, but before you knew it, you would end up eating popcorn off each other. You could reach for the coke bottle in their hand, but sometime before the interval, they would reach for your hand. And you would be powerless to resist.

By the time the end credits rolled, it would be your end too. You'd leave the theatre wondering how you went from holding hands to cupping each other's face to locking lips to . . .

Hey, don't look at me like that. You tell me. If the guy of your dreams wanted to kiss your face, would you turn it away? If the lust of your life made a pass at you, would you pass up the opportunity? You would? Congratulations! Now please get your hormones tested. I'm sorry, but I'm normal.

After the movie, when TJ was driving me back home, I turned to him and said, 'I think it's safe to say that our friendship is effectively ruined.'

Like Monica had told Chandler after they hooked up in England. I was half hoping he would say the same thing Chandler had: 'Nah, we weren't that good friends, anyway.'

Instead, he murmured, 'That was always the plan, baby, that was always the plan.' He didn't even take his eyes off the road.

Don't ask about my eyes. They were all goggled. My ears were ringing. My stomach was bearing the brunt of the butterflies that had broken into a vigorous song and dance routine.

Everything was the same after the movie. Everything was different after that movie.

My parents didn't morph into considerate, cool or lenient beings. But I could filter their voices out so much more effectively. Thinking of the time I'd spent with TJ came to my rescue.

My teachers didn't make learning fun, exciting or bearable. But I could tune them out effortlessly. Looking forward to the next time we'd be together came to my aid.

I didn't become more attractive, slim or interesting. I just felt I had. Repeating all the things TJ said to me helped.

I had written them down in my secret diary so I could read, reread and memorize them. Just thinking about them gave me gooseflesh. It felt so good being one half of a madly-into-each-other couple. And the 'L' word hadn't even been said yet.

Unbelievably Romantic Things Tejas Said To Me

....
....
....

Sorry! Way too personal, guys.:)

Suffice to say, for the next two months, I had only one thing on my mind. I was like one of those man-eating tigers they show on National Geographic Channel. Once they taste blood, they can't go back to eating deer.

Too bad his mum was back and we couldn't use his pad. I bet his elder bro could have used more of TLC. Anyway, it just meant visiting more theatres and watching more flop movies (ideal for privacy).

On days I had to attend college (because TJ had to attend his) I was like a yogi, intent on my goal. I was calm, collected and controlled. Even when a group of seniors came and dragged a bunch of us out on election duty. Even when we went from department to department chanting 'Srilatha for College President'. Even when we extolled her virtues—leadership, compassion, courage—to the classrooms bursting with students.

It would have been a different matter had anyone asked me to point Srilatha out. I couldn't care less about the B.Com department's presidential candidate.

I'm sure the election results were out in September (and someone must have won). I'm sure several events of national importance transpired that month (our president must have travelled abroad at least once). I'm sure it was an eventful month, internationally even (Lindsay Lohan must have gone to jail at least once).

But I simply wasn't interested. All I wanted was to get away from the world and launch myself into TJ's arms. But he had a college to attend.

Cut off as I was from the rest of the world, I soon became aware of a dumb new traffic rule in Chennai. No tinted glasses. Cops were catching people, forcing them to strip their cars off them.

'Great, just great!' I'd cribbed on one matinee date when TJ's car showed up minus the protective film. 'Just when I started going around.'

'Relax, Rinks. You worry too much.'

'But TJ, you don't understand.'

But he had laughed and silenced me, cough, cough, the only way he could.

Heart-warming as these Public Displays of Affection were, I had to be very, very careful. I couldn't afford getting caught by the wolf pack. Robin, I could imagine how she'd react. But no saying how Google and Adit (not that I cared about *his* opinion) would.

Thank God Ankita was out of my life. There was no fooling that babe. Anks was like a walking-talking microscope. One look and she could tell what base a person had gone up to. I mean, she could have ghostwritten the *Kamasutra*. Plus, she had her lawyer dad's interrogatory skills.

Robin and Sudha, not so much. They were far, far easier to fool. They'd dropped in one Friday afternoon (yeah, after bunking college) and I'd managed to conduct an entire conversation with TJ on the landline, passing him off as Google!

When Tejas called again later that night and I narrated the whole episode to him, he dismissed it as 'silly'. Said I was crazy to keep things from my friends. And he accused me of, hold your breath, treating him like a dirty secret.

As if dating a hottie could ever be something to be ashamed of.

They say most couples fight over money, parents, shopping. Ladies and gentlemen, kindly add friends to that list.

TJ just didn't get it. I guess he was just being a *guy*. It's not as if I enjoyed playing a cat and mouse game with my wolf pack. It's just that it was too early in our relationship (this time around, I wanted only two people in it).

We were getting to know each other (and I don't only mean physically, don't be gross). Naturally I wanted to treat the phase as an exquisite piece of lingerie: hold it close to my heart, relish how it made me feel, and yeah, keep it private.

The last thing I wanted was to face an interrogation squad. I knew my friends as well as TJ knew his video games. They'd go completely ballistic. Oh, yeah. They would ask a million questions, throw tons of reasons why TJ was bad news, why we were all wrong for each other. Maybe we were. But I just wanted to find out for myself. And I must confess, I was having a blast figuring things out.

Why was that so hard for him to understand?

Things were different with his friends, of course. Like a swarm of mosquitoes, they were almost always around. Initially at his house parties, and when we started seeing each other, at Rocco, the afternoon discotheque we frequented.

It was such a poor excuse of a disc. Sheer waste of space, time and money. Horrible short-eats, bad lighting and the music—the flops of the Eighties, each time we went there. But people with late night issues had to make do with the next best thing. Sigh.

BTW, a strange thing happened at Rocco. I bumped into a college classmate, Sundari. She recognized *me*. Would you believe, Sundari spent the entire afternoon wrapping herself like a python around random guys. The next time I went to college, I was shocked to see her sitting in the first row. And they say the girls who sit in the last row are fast.

Anyway, spending time with TJ made me realize my feelings. Not for him. For Adit and Google. They were so not boyfriend material. Not *my* boyfriend material, for sure. Oh, they were great guys. Amazing friends. Yeah, even Adit. Now that I had TJ in my life, I could afford to be magnanimous. But I'd been crazy to date them. We just didn't have *that*, you know. The spark I felt with TJ. To be completely honest, in TJ's case, it was no spark. It was a mile-high flame.

There was another difference. With the boys, I could be myself. Totally. I could act all silly, let my hair down, eat like a pig. Do all the crazy stuff I'd never do in front of Tejas, not in a million years. Hey, I didn't want him to think I was weird. Or imperfect. Or worse, not girlfriend material. Precisely why I couldn't take him into confidence when the next big crisis erupted in my life.

Movie Genre of the Week: Romantic

Rinki's Top 10:

1. *Pretty Woman*
2. *Kuch Kuch Hota Hai*
3. *Hum Tum*
4. *When Harry Met Sally*
5. *Love Aaj Kal*
6. *Notting Hill*
7. *Love Actually*
8. *Dilwale Dulhania Le Jayenge*
9. *Dil Toh Pagal Hai*
10. *The Notebook*

Chapter 16

RinkiTripathi@ChennaiSuperChick
Gandhigiri or Goondagiri? When in doubt, go with option B.

It was November, months since my stint at *Divaa*. I'd all but forgotten about my time there.

But one Saturday night at The Backyard, it all came flooding back. I was leafing through Neha's copy of the magazine when I came across an ad. An innocuous looking ad for a jewellery store. I read it twice. Then I read it one more time. I couldn't put a finger on it but something was not right.

Just then, Adit walked in. I tossed the magazine aside.

'What's he doing here?' I said, springing to my feet.

'Rinki, relax,' Adit began. 'You're being ridiculous.'

'Oh, yeah? Says who?'

'Our cold war has gone on long enough.'

'Let me be the judge of that, Adit. Googs, why did you call this guy? You know how I feel about him. About backstabbers.'

Google poured a large rum and cola for himself and tossed us a 'Go club each other to death, for all I care' look.

'I did not backstab you, Rinki. You did not want to be friends with me. As simple as that. Yes, we should have run it past you. We made a mistake and for that, we're genuinely sorry. It's been months. Can't you put all that behind you? Can't you just be happy for us?'

'Arrrrrrrrghhhhhh!' I let out a war cry and jumped to my feet. Adit recoiled and covered his face with the back of his hands.

Hey, I wasn't about to lynch Adit. I'd finally figured out what was bothering me. It was the ad in *Divaa*. The slogan, to be precise. It was mine. And it'd been published. The month before last. And I hadn't heard from TB. Not a squeak. The sneak!

'Hey, hey, hey,' Google butt in. 'Why all the Sunny paaji aggression?'

'A douchebag published my slogan and didn't pay me for it, that's why.'

Adit's hands dropped to his side. Did he really think I'd attack him?

'Are you sure, Rinks?' Adit asked.

'Sure, confident, lock it,' I snapped, flinging the magazine in his direction.

'Does Neha subscribe to the magazine?'

Google nodded.

'Could you get all the earlier copies, please?' Adit instructed, appointing himself in charge.

Google ran down to get hold of them.

We leafed through the issues. Sure enough, there they were. My slogans. In every single issue for the last few months. The cheap, conniving, two-bit, double-faced @#$%.

'Time to pay TB a visit,' I declared, wiping my mouth with the back of my hand.

'Trust me, Rinki. Don't bother going to his office. Such guys don't understand words, they only understand this,' Google said, bunching his fingers into a fist.

'Since when did you become a Shaolin Master? Shut up and go back to your drink,' Adit admonished him. 'Rinki, don't listen to him. Violence only breeds violence.'

'Okay, Mahatma Adit, kindly advise us on the next course of action.'

Adit advised me to call TB. Demand an explanation. Surely there would be one.

Over the next few days, I did. But each time, he was either:

1. Busy
2. Out of office
3. Travelling

Two weeks later, I was still wringing my hands. Mails had gone unanswered. So had repeated calls. It was driving me up the wall. I really wanted to go barging into his office and collect the cash. And some of his teeth as interest.

Google was with me. But Adit being Adit was proposing the peaceful alternative. We'd kind of made up during that Backyard session. And he was back to acting as the Voice of Reason in my life.

'Let's go and have a friendly chat with him,' he suggested.

'Yes, Adit,' Google agreed, looking up from his comic. 'You play the good cop. I'll play the bad cop.'

'Shut up, Google. We won't do anything of that sort.

We'll just put our thoughts across the table in a dignified, decent manner.'

'We?' I asked.

'Yes, we,' Adit and Google chorused firmly.

Not that I needed any support but I gamely agreed to take the boys along.

At the foyer of TB's office, I developed cold feet. 'What if he refuses to meet me?'

There was a new face at the front desk. 'From?' she asked us brusquely.

'*Hawa Hawai Magazine*.'

I shot Google a furious look. Hawa Hawai, seriously?

Google rolled up a newspaper and shot me a 'whatever' look.

We cooled our heels for a few tense minutes.

'Please go in,' Front desk Lady said presently.

I got to my feet gingerly.

TB was wearing a full-sleeved black T-shirt with the slogan 'I am a Diva. I am a Goddess'.

Strange, the words seemed so familiar. Had I read it some place? A mail someone had forwarded? An FB share? Then it struck me. They were my words. MY WORDS. He had said my slogans had been rejected. All of them. Yet, here he was wearing one of them on a T-shirt. Bas@#$%!

I wanted to lunge across the table, catch him by the collar and haul him up. Like they do on those Z-grade action movies on HBO. But he seemed at least a hundred and fifty kilos heavier than me.

'Rinki? Mala said someone from Hawai magazine were here to meet me. Anyway, tell me, tell me,' he said, glancing at his watch.

Oh, he was Mr Busy Bee, was he? Busy being a robber, more like.

I got straight to the point.

'TB, back when I'd joined *Divaa*, you'd promised to give me thousand bugs, er bucks, for each published slogan.'

He pushed his aviators further up his nose. 'Really? Did I? Doesn't ring a bell.'

Perhaps if I hit him with a bell, things would be clearer.

Google spoke up. 'Let's cut to the chase, TB Baby. You owe our friend moolah. Out with it.'

'And who might you be?' TB asked, swinging around to look at Google.

'Might be? Heylooo, I exist. Don't doubt it. It's a fact.'

'Huh?' A look of sheer bewilderment came over TB's face.

'TB, please don't mind our friend. What he means to say is, you owe Rinki money. For all the slogans she's written for you.' It was Adit's turn to speak up.

'And who are you?'

'Her bodyguards,' Google supplied.

'Bodyguards?' TB's eyes narrowed. He settled back into his chair, an amused look on his face. 'I see.'

I coughed. 'Look, TB, let's not waste any more time. Just pay me for the slogans and we'll be on our way. I've spend enough time chasing you as it is.'

'That's because I was travelling.'

'So was the rest of the office?' I asked acerbically.

'You know it is a one-man show, Rinki. I need to be around to do everything.'

Yeah, especially to write slogans.

'Well, you are back now. May I have my money?'

'Let me see,' he said rifling through a couple of papers like a sham master. 'Hey, why don't you mail me?'

'No, TB, I have been waiting for you to mail me for the—'

'—last few months,' he said completing my sentence. 'But I was travelling.'

'Well, you are not now,' I asserted.

'Let me see . . .' he said, trailing off, punching some keys on the keyboard.

Wow, this could take all day.

'Rinki, why don't you give me a day and I'll get back to you.'

I was soooo pissed, I wanted to break the ugly porcelain pigeon set lying on his desk on his head.

I guess Adit could read my mind. He flashed me a look that said, 'No use antagonizing the man further.'

I guess Google could read my mind, too. Because when he got to his feet and whirled around to leave, his hand brushed past the porcelain pigeon set and sent it flying.

Smash!!!

We didn't wait to see the million pieces that became of it.

Back at The Backyard, I drew up a list of things we could do. Desired Action: Make the jerk pay up.

Options open:

    a. Discussion. Door closed.

    b. Intimidation. To be considered.

    c. Write off payment as bad debt. Chance illa. No chance.

       I'd bloody worked my ass off on the slogans.

'Should have known that guy wasn't all right. What's with those idiotic aviators? And who wears full-sleeves, machan?' Google wondered aloud.

'Pratibha Patil,' Sudha answered sombrely.

'Any of you know any goondas?' I asked looking around.

Sudha looked as if the biggest goonda she'd ever come across was me. Adit shifted uncomfortably.

Google filled his vodka glass with ice cubes. 'I'll ask Chhotoo. He's this big muscular guy in my college.'

A big muscular dude called Chhotoo. Wow, sounded really promising.

I was mighty irritated. I'd done nothing wrong. I'd worked hard. Submitted my work on time. TB had made money off it. But he was just refusing to pay. It was plain wrong. But there was nothing I could do about it.

I was angry with myself. How could I have let this happen?

I was angry with my parents too. How could they have let me work? Didn't they know it was a big bad world out there? Wasn't it their duty to protect me from the wolves? Surely Dad knew some loan sharks who could just land up at AB's doorstep and snatch money from him?

I was angry with my country. What sort of a country lets its labour force get exploited? Where were those trade unions when we needed them?

I was angry with the media. There they were, the anchorpersons, shouting at hapless panelists in the air-conditioned comfort of the studio when they should have been by my side. Exposing TB's cheapness. Making it the breaking news of the day.

Robin, who'd been awfully quiet, spoke up. 'I'll talk to my maid. She always keeps mentioning this don type of character who lives in her shanty.'

Adit groaned. 'Robin, listen to yourself! We're decent people. We don't hire goondas to settle our scores.'

'Yeah,' I said heatedly. 'We are people who sit quietly and let others rob us blind.'

'Trust me, Rinki. I'm damn angry at that ass#$%@ too.'

Wow, Adit was abusing. He was actually using a cuss word. For me. That was sweet. It was enough to warm the cockles (whatever they are) of my heart.

'I want to help you, too, Rinki. I just don't know how,' Adit continued.

'Sue that basket, I say,' Googled hollered. 'Anyone know a good lawyer?'

Adit and I exchanged a glance. We knew one with a highly resourceful daughter. Ohhhhmyyygod!

'Why didn't I think of it earlier!' I cried out.

'Because you were not exactly on proper terms with Ankita,' Adit reminded me softly.

Proper terms. It was a euphemism. I'd been ignoring Ankita for months. Refusing to take her calls.

And now, when I needed her help, was I ready to put everything behind me? For six thousand bucks? The little voice in my head reminded me. But it was *six thousand* bucks. There was so much I could do with that kind of money. Question was, would I get my due? Surely I could swallow my pride and go crawling back to Ankita, my BFF turned

BFF (Best Foe Forever). And that made me feel terrible. I wish I had given her a chance. Without needing to give her a chance.

Movie Genre of the Week: Suspense

Rinki's Top 10:

1. *Memento*
2. *The Prestige*
3. *Talaash*
4. *Humraaz*
5. *Gupt*
6. *Zodiac*
7. *Kahaani*
8. *Gone Baby Gone*
9. *The Sixth Sense*
10. *Mulholland Drive*

Chapter 17

RinkiTripathi@ChennaiSuperChick
The tastiest dish in the world? Revenge. Served cold.

'Rinks?'

Gosh! It was Anks.

'Anks!'

'Hi Rinks,' she began awkwardly. 'Adit just called me.'

Oh God. What would she think? Now that I needed her, I was all ready and willing to talk to her? Listen to her side of things?

'Anks, look . . .'

Ankita cut me off mid-sentence. 'Rinks, forget all that happened in the past.'

'I want to, Anks.'

'Look, I'm sorry, Rinks. I'm soooo soooo soooo sorry. Swear. Promise. Cross my heart. I never meant to hurt you. I know I screwed up. I should have cleared it out with you first. I didn't mean to go behind your back. I didn't want you to find out the way you did. And for that I'm really really really, to the power of thousand, sorry. Forgive me, please?'

'Oh, Anks,' I sniffed, choking back tears. 'I don't want to you to think that I'm doing this only because I need your help.'

'Are you MAD?' Anks bellowed. 'You'd never do that. Because you're one stubborn pigheaded bizz!'

'That I am,' I chuckled.

And just like that, the floodgates opened up and we poured our hearts to each other.

'Wow, Anks, you must really love Adit. You and long distance. You and long-term. Who would have thought. It's been, what, six months, since you and Adit have been together?'

'Even my jeans don't last that long,' Ankita said in equal amazement.

'It must be love,' I said in admiration.

'I don't know, Rinks. It's complicated. Adit is not like the other guys.'

'You mean, like those Delhi creeps you've dated in the past.'

'They weren't creeps,' Ankita protested half-heartedly.

'Well, not all of them. Some were just complete freaks.'

'Well, if you put it that way,' Ankita averred.

We chuckled.

'Oh, Anks, it's so good to talk to you.'

'You too, babe, you too. Okay, enough about me. Now tell me about that a@# who's been troubling you."

I brought her up to speed.

'Hmmm,' Anks said at last. 'Let me think. I'm sure something will come up.'

'I don't know what to do, Anks,' I said, wringing my hands. 'I feel so stupid.'

'Calm down, Rinks. I have an idea. Here's what we'll do.'

I went over Ankita's plan in my mind. Gosh, it was perfect. I was so so so thrilled. I was going to get my money back. Oh, yeah. I wanted to see the look on that jackass's face when . . .

I was so busy making castles in the air that I didn't hear my castle, er, room's door open.

Mom and Dad were standing there, hands on their hips, identical (not to mention, gravest of grave) Rinki-how-could-you-do-this-to-us expressions on their faces.

'What did I do now?' I asked them in exasperation.

I knew that if Mom spoke up, it'd be something trivial. But if Dad did, hoo boy, I was in deep shite. I'd been in a soup often enough to know as much. So who'd it be? I held my breath.

Dad opened his mouth and I groaned.

'Rinki, since when have you started roaming around with rowdies?'

What? Me and rowdies? Limited as my dating options were, I had my standards.

Mom ambled over and sat down on the bed heavily.

'We're getting calls from strangers. Telling us our daughter has become a goondi.'

'Don't exaggerate, Sheena. It was just one call. This gentleman . . .'

'Dad, how could he possibly be a gentleman if he's spreading tales about an innocent little girl?'

'Obviously, if you keep the company of rowdies, you'll also turn into one.'

'What on earth are you talking about, Mom? What's all this Rowdy Rathore drama?'

Dad took a deep breath. Uh-oh.

'Rinki, we just got a call from this gentleman. He said you've going to places, henchmen in tow, breaking things, threatening people and demanding money.'

I suddenly had visions of me dressed like Munnabhai, collecting hafta from unsuspecting shopkeepers. The sight of Robin dressed as Circuit, black kurta pyjama and golden chains made me giggle.

'See, she's laughing. Oh my God, my one and only daughter has turned into a goondi.'

That's when it hit me. They were talking about me and Google and Adit.

TB had called my house. My house! The nerve. How the hell did he get his hands on my number? The tattling, bean-spilling whistle-blowing swine! Just when I was trying to keep my family out of the whole ugly mess.

And then I remembered. My resume. Of course. Bloody hell!

'Dad, that was no gentleman on the phone. It was that @#$% TB,' I hollered.

'Rinki,' Dad said sharply. 'I won't have that kind of language in my house.'

'Sorry, Dad, but just hear me out. Please?'

Dad settled down next to Mom. And when I finished, Mom exploded. 'That @#$%!'

My point exactly.

'Rinki, I understand,' Dad spoke up.

Did he now? So why wasn't he getting ready to jump into a car and go threaten TB? Mom looked willing enough.

'It's totally wrong on the part of that gentleman . . .'

That word again. Grrr!

'. . . to withhold payment for services rendered,' Dad continued. 'It's completely unethical and unprofessional. However, that does not give us a licence to act in a rash manner. What I suggest is that we wait it out. Let's be patient and see. Who knows, perhaps he will come around? Clear your dues, without so much as a rude reminder.'

Yeah, right. And politicians will go around the streets of our country distributing thousand-rupee notes to the poor.

'Stop giving her a lecture. Tell us how to get our money back,' Mom hissed.

'Er, did you just say "our money", Mom?'

'Of course! Don't you know? It's an old Indian tradition. Children always give their first salaries to their mothers.'

Funny, I'd never known Mom to be a traditional Bharatiya nari.

Dad got to his feet. 'Think about my suggestions, ladies. Give it time. TB will call you and ask you to pick up the money himself. Trust me, it will all work out.'

That's what Europe had thought about Hitler.

'By the way, how much does he owe you?'

'Six thousand rupees, Dad.'

'Six thousand rupees?' Mom gasped. 'I could easily buy a nice saree from Nalli with that.'

Right then, I made a deal with God. If he helped me get it back, I'd gladly sacrifice it on a technicolour saree.

As revenge dramas go, it was pretty simple. All I'd to do was follow Ankita's instructions to the T.

Find out TB's weakness.

Catch him red-handed.

Have incontrovertible proof.

Grist mills at *Divaa* magazine had been agog with the rumour: TB's drinking problem. He'd been warned on several occasions. By the owners of the publishing house that ran *Divaa*, no less.

His poison? Whiskey on the rocks. Yeah, El Cheapo had expensive tastes. No wonder he needed to sponge off interns.

By a stroke of luck, I was in possession of the proof. I'd stumbled upon it in all innocence. Here's how. On my last day, I'd borrowed Dad's iPad. To shoot an office video. A part of my preserve-all-memories drive.

Armed with the gizmo, I'd gone from desk to desk, from work floor to lunch room. Covering every nook and corner.

Last stop, TB's room. I'd assumed he'd stepped out for lunch as usual. I'd just about turned the handle when two loud gasps rend the air. Mine and TB's. My free hand flew to my mouth. There was TB, his legs propped up, taking a leisurely sip of whiskey, a Chivas Regal bottle lying open on his desk.

I'd mumbled a loud 'Oops', done a Scooby Doo style about-turn out of the room. But not before the iPad had captured everything for posterity. His caught-with-knickers-down expression, the glass, the bottle, the ice bucket, everything.

The video clip was safely tucked away. All I'd to do was forward it. To TB's cell phone. And I did.

Ankita had directed me to add a sweet little message as well. 'Hi TB! Hope all is well. Look what I found. Would love to hear the management's thoughts on this. Take care, Rinki.'

Oh, I was confident. The picture would speak a thousand bucks. Make that six thousand bucks.

Sure enough, he pinged me instantly. 'How much do we owe you again, Rinki?'

And the very next day, an envelope containing six crisp thousand rupee notes was hand delivered to my house by TB's driver.

Anks-Rinks Jodi Number One had conquered the world yet again. The wolf pack (with Anks on the speakerphone) celebrated the grand success of Operation Paisa Vasool at The Backyard. With a bottle of, you guessed it, Chivas Regal.

Movie Genre of the Week: Spy Thrillers

Rinki's Top Ten:
1. *North by Northwest*
2. *The Constant Gardener*
3. *The Bourne Supremacy*
4. *Hanna*
5. *Ek Tha Tiger*
6. *Agent Vinod*
7. *Mission Impossible: Ghost Protocol*
8. *Munich*
9. *True Lies*
10. *Knight and Day*

Chapter 18

RinkiTripathi@ChennaiSuperChick
Very very Pondicherry. Oui!

Every college has at least one boring tradition that you CANNOT duck. No matter how hard you try. CWC, for instance, had the annual college trip. Each year, they'd ferry the students to some of the most borrrring places on earth. And the places never changed. I bet if you asked the Class of 1950 where they went, their answer would be:

1. Ooty
2. Kodai Kanal
3. Bengaluru-Mysuru

As if there weren't any other interesting places on earth.

As the year drew to a close, Killjoy Option #3 was announced for the Class of 2012.

So the wolf pack decided to start a tradition all of their own.

Like all madcap ideas, it was Google's. Over drinks at The Backyard, he suggested we duck the college trip and head to

Pondi (for the uninitiated, that's Pondicherry, the little slice of France, tucked away about two hours away from Chennai).

It was settled. B'lore was out. Pondi was in.

As expected, Robin tried to wiggle her way out.

'Robin, please,' I began. 'You can come back and study all you want for the annual exams.' They were not until March, for God's sake.

'I don't know, Rinks.'

'Robin, look, we get study leave all of Feb.'

'Sriram might come down in Feb.'

So that's what it was. I couldn't believe how clingy Sriram was acting. He was always coming to Chennai, getting in the way, pouring water over my well-laid plans.

Sigh. Robin had left me with no other choice. It was time to pull out the big guns.

'Remember when I gave you the makeover, Robin? You called me your Style Guru. Well, your Guru wants her dakshina. Now.'

Last year, when she'd just about started dating Sriram, I'd waved my magic wand and lo! Robin Isaac Version 2.0 was born.

She opened her mouth but I held up a hand.

'No excuses. I demand my dakshina. Only, I want you to pay it in kind. By coming with me to Pondi.'

Robin looked exceedingly pained but had the decency to keep quiet.

One battle won.

On to the most important battle. One that would win the war. Taking care of the parents bit. My brain was in fifth gear. I felt like those FBI guys on that Star World show *Criminal*

Minds. Thinking each move through, always one step ahead in the game.

'Girls, let's stick to the same story. That we're going on a college trip to Bengaluru. Only, we'll go to Pondicherry. We'll be back in three days. Easy peasy. Trust me, our folks won't have a clue. And what they don't know . . .'

'. . . cannot hurt them,' Sudha finished like a well-trained puppy. Attagirl.

'You know you would make a good lawyer, Rinki Tripathi,' Robin observed.

Devil's advocate, more like.

Cut to the second week of December.

We were welcomed at Villa Helena by a power cut.

'Today light gone only for four hours,' the caretaker, Mr Jumbolingam ('Call me Jumbo, childrens') informed us, flashing his yellow teeth.

'I don't know about you guys but my light has gone for the rest of the day,' I quipped, plopping down on the nearest available couch.

The gang proceeded to call folks back home.

Mom had lent me her Blackberry. Trust me, there was nothing altruistic about the gesture. Dad said he wanted me to be reachable. Ha! It was just another way of keeping an eye on their offspring. But I wasn't complaining. Not in the slightest. Armed with a cell phone, I could put regular updates on BBM, FB and Twitter.

After assurances that we were all fine and the weather was just great in Bengaluru, we assembled in the sprawling living room. I'd sworn to myself I wouldn't call TJ (we'd had a lover's tiff).

The place was beautiful. The furniture was all antique, the drapes were sheer and colourful artefacts adorned the room. I guess it would have been lovely with the wonders of modern science. Like electricity and generators.

'What's so great about Pondi?' I grumbled, scratching my leg as another mosquito attacked it.

'I don't know about you but I love Paandi,' Google squealed, doing his firang accent.

'Thank you, childrens,' Mr Jumbo said with an exaggerated bow, clearly overwhelmed.

I couldn't wait to get out of the villa. And I would've had Adit not come down with a bad case of food poisoning. He spent the rest of the day in the washroom, drawing pitying looks from all of us. Except his roommate.

'Gross! Disgusting! I cannot, WILL NOT share my room with that,' Google protested, way more upset than Adit's stomach. But he had little choice.

Neha and I were bunking in one room; Robin and Sudha in the other.

Luckily for Adit, Robin was carrying her medicine pouch. Too bad, the pill took its own sweet time to work. It was evening by the time Adit felt slightly better.

There was nothing much to be done. So the gang decided to stay in and play cards. Though the stakes were modest, the Varma siblings, emerged considerably rich at the end of the session. Guess gambling runs in the genes.

The next day dawned bright and sunny. All of us were up by noon.

'Let's go to Auroville, people! They have a lovely meditation centre there,' Robin suggested.

'Yes, lovely. Robin, why don't you leave immediately? Go, scat, shoo,' Google growled.

Robin made a sulky face.

'For the rest of us, I've got a rocking idea,' Google continued. 'Why don't we hit a disc/nightclub/pub this evening?'

'Googs, you're in Pondicherry not Ibiza,' I reminded him.

'Hmm, I'd love a pizza,' Adit said, emerging from, where else, the washroom.

'Really?' Google said, his voice laced with sarcasm. 'If I were you, I'd be on a diet of curd rice, machan. For the rest of the month.'

'Guys, how about we go for a leisurely lunch and then a walk on the beach in the evening?' Robin suggested.

That drew loud cheers from all around. We drove past White Town, the loveliest part of Pondicherry. It felt as if we weren't in India at all. It was that quaint and quiet. That peaceful and pretty.

After a hearty meal of yummy spaghetti, spicy meatballs, cheesy wood-fired pizzas and out-of-this-world tiramisu at a tiny restaurant run by a chatty Frenchman and his charming wife, everyone slid down lower in the chairs.

*Story behind the lover's tiff

I'd made plans to go to Fisherman's Cove with Tejas that same weekend. Fish Cove, the ultra swank resort on East Coast Road. Its restaurants were packed to capacity around the year. TJ had to pull major strings to get us a table.

Two plans. One weekend. I wanted to kick myself. What a predicament. I mulled over the options. Sigh. I could always go to Fish Cove with TJ some other time but opportunities like Pondi don't come by often.

'Tejas?'

'Good morning, beautiful.'

Aww, I was going to give him the ditch and he was being so sweet.

'TJ, got a minute?'

'For you, Rinks, all the time in the world,' Tejas drawled.

Yeah, right. I'd remind him the next time he was hooked on to his stupid video games.

'Um, TJ, I was just wondering if I could take a rain check for the Fish Cove weekend?'

'Hey, everything okay?'

Shoot, didn't mean to worry him.

'Hey, it's all good. It's just that the gang is planning a trip to Pondi. And I'd very much like to go. My college trip is around the same time, so it's a god-sent opportunity for me. I can get out of home, no questions asked,' I explained, the words tumbling out of my mouth.

'Have fun, babe,' TJ said without missing a beat. 'When do you leave?'

Apparently, a little jealousy was too much to ask for. I guess not all boyfriends could be as clingy as Sriram.

But a girl could live in her fantasy world, couldn't she.

Movie Genre of the Week: Fantasy

Rinki's Top 10:

1. *The Lord of the Rings: The Fellowship of the Ring*
2. *Harry Potter and the Deathly Hallows*
3. *Chronicles of Narnia: The Lion, The Witch and The Wardrobe*
4. *Eragon*
5. *Pan's Labyrinth*
6. *Avatar*
7. *Enchanted*
8. *Bridge to Terabithia*
9. *Twilight: Breaking Dawn*
10. *Alice in Wonderland*

Chapter 19

**RinkiTripathi@ChennaiSuperChick
What's your favourite fruit? Mine's forbidden.**

It was half past four by the time we reached the rocky beach. We went and flopped down next to the steps of Gandhi Madapam. The others were content to survey the ocean of humanity that had congregated at the promenade. I, however, lost no time in updating my BBM status.

Sudha reached for Robin's hand. Google grinned wolfishly at me. I was about to shoot him a don't-even-think-about-it' look. But then I thought heck, why the hell not.

Without warning, three snazzy looking bikes (later Google mentioned they were modified Bullets) roared on to the street. They zipped closer and closer with a deafening sound and braked at the Gandhi Memorial, inches away from where we stood.

One of the bikers whipped off his helmet, shaking out his luxuriant hair like an exotic shampoo model.

He fished out a piece of paper from his jacket and went, 'Excuse me, could you tell me where Hotel La Dupleix is, please?'

Bloooooooooodyyy hell! It was Tejas! What the hell was he doing in Pondi????

'T-T-Tejas?' I squawked, extricating my arm from Google's in a flash.

'Ohmyygod, Tripthi? Is that you?' Tejas gawped, doing the best overacting of his career.

Yeah, right, Mr Ham Actor of the Year.

'So, we meet again,' Tejas purred, a devilish gleam in his eye.

Five hostile pairs of eyes swung in my direction. I could just imagine what was going on in their heads.

What the hell is he doing here—Robin

Google would look so much better in that leather jacket—Sudha

Rinki, our local Tigress Woods—Adit

Rinki knows boys who look like *that*—Neha

I've got to get me one of those (bikes, that is)—Google

'W-w-what are you doing here?' I blubbered, unable to believe my eyes. 'I mean, imagine bumping into you at Pondi,' I improvised quickly.

'What are the chances, right?' TJ said sweetly.

I just stood there gaping at him. My first thought: my clothes! Mercifully, I was wearing my pink sundress and matching flip-flops, my new hoops and beads. My second thought: had he followed me to Pondi? Ohmygoooood. He had. He had followed me. He had sounded so cool on the phone. I should have known.

What the hell was he trying to do? Was he trying to get back at me? For ditching out on the Fish Cove weekend. Trying to expose me in front of my friends? The jerk! I was never going to speak to him again.

'Where are your manners, Rinki?' TJ cut into my thoughts. 'Aren't you going to introduce me to your friends?'

He was such a pig.

'Of course. Robin and Sudha you already know.'

'Girls,' Tejas acknowledged them.

The girls stood there stiffly.

'Neha, meet Tejas. He was our senior at CBVB.'

'Hi, Neha,' Tejas flashed her an impish grin.

'How you doin'?' Neha shot back, her head cocked to one side.

I rolled my eyes before introducing him to the boys.

'That's Adit.'

'Hi,' Adit muttered, without so much as extending his hand.

'And that's Google.'

'Cowboy,' Google nodded at him, touching the tip of his imaginary hat.

The corners of TJ's mouth twitched.

Yeah, as if his friends, Arun, Deepak and their dumb girlfriends were perfect. One big vicious circle his social circle was.

'So, what are you doing here, Tejas?' Robin asked pointedly.

That's when panic set in. Robin was a smart cookie. Five more minutes in his company and she'd put two and two together.

'Here for the weekend with some friends,' he gestured in the direction of his biker buddies.

'Wait a minute, your name sounds awfully familiar, Tejas,' Adit mused.

Shoot! Had Ankita told him about our history?

'Really?' Tejas asked Adit, a dangerous tell-me-more expression on his face. 'Been telling tales out of school, Tripthi?'

Google couldn't contain himself. 'Who the hell is Tripthi?'

'Gosh!' I said loudly, clapping the dial on my watch. 'Is that the time? We better head back.'

'Nice meeting you, guys. It's been what, a year since we last met?' Tejas drawled. 'School farewell, remember?'

'You forgot the ragging session at the railway tracks,' Sudha reminded him diligently.

I put my hands on Sudha's back and shoved her in the opposite direction.

'Sure you don't want me to drop you somewhere?'

Me hop on to his bike? I could just imagine the looks on my friends' faces.

'Umm, no. Bye, Tejas.'

'Bye, Rinki,' Tejas said.

He put his helmet back on and with a crisp salute disappeared in a cloud of dust.

Everyone's mind was working in overdrive. I could practically hear them.

'Is everyone thinking what I am thinking?' Google spoke up.

I opened my mouth to set the record straight.

'Time for *pet puja*, right?' he asked, patting his stomach.

'Shut up, Google,' everyone chorused.

'Okay, who wants to go first?' I ventured bravely.

'Rinki, what's going on . . .'

'Who the hell is that guy . . .'

'What was that about . . .'

'Stopppppp!' I screamed.

Everyone fell silent.

'Guys, shoot! One at a time, please.'

Adit went first. 'Who was that guy?'

'Tejas, my senior from school.'

'God, he's dishy!' Neha swooned. 'He's like sex on toast!'

Remember Ajay, Neha? Your boyfriend?

Google waved his hand.

'Yes, Googs?'

'What's he doing in Paandi, Rinki?'

'Same thing we are, Google. Chilling with friends. You heard the guy.'

'I don't buy it,' Robin said flatly.

'What's not to buy? It's a small world. People bump into each other all the time,' I said impassively.

'So you haven't been meeting him on the sly?' Robin asked through narrowed eyes.

'Robin! Don't you trust me?'

She shook her head. Oh Robin, you're so right not to.

'You'd tell us if something was brewing, right?' Sudha asked timidly.

'Sure I would,' I said sincerely.

Yeah, and politicians would stop lying.

Robin launched her favourite spiel: the unsuitability of one Mr Tejas for one Miss Rinki. Sudha recounted everything that had happened back in Class 11.

Very soon, Neha, Adit and Google had joined the 'Don't even think about him' clamour. I put on my best 'Don't know what you're talking about' expression.

'Guys, guys, guys,' I implored. 'I'm not that dumb. I know better than to make the same mistake twice. Promise I don't have the hots for Tejas. Swear I'll never have anything to do with him.' I pinched the skin of my throat solemnly.

Of course, I said 'Promise toothpaste' under my breath. So I wasn't actually lying.

It seemed to have the desired effect on them.

'Fine, Rinki. If you say so,' they said in unison.

Thank you, God, for getting them off my back.

We had an early day ahead. Plus, there was packing to be done. So everyone decided turn in early. Neha was out the second her bed hit the pillow.

Five minutes after I switched off the overhead light, I launched into the mini war.

Where are you, TJ?

At La Dupleix. Good dinner. Join me for dessert?

I ignored that. *What was all that about?*

What you talking about, Rinks?

That bike stunt you pulled!

Liked it?

Stoopppp it! TJ, how could you? WHAT were you thinking!

I was just thinking how long it had been since I last saw you.

It's not been long at all. We met last week.

So? A guy's not allowed to miss his girlfriend?

Fine, be flippant, TJ. I was so mad at him. I didn't text back for one whole minute.

Trips? You there? Look, I'm sorry.

You don't mean that, TJ. You did it on purpose. You wanted to make trouble. And you succeeded. Happy now?

I was happy seeing your face. But obviously, you weren't.

How could I? With my friends' gaze boring holes into me.

So, what are you wearing right now? The night suit with the dolphins?

I was. Like hell I'd give him the satisfaction of knowing he was right.

Trips, come on. I know you're there.

My fingers didn't budge.

Who was that guy again? The one whose hand you were holding?

Hell! He had noticed!

It was Google, it was nothing.

Chill, Trips! I was just kidding.

That's the problem, TJ. You're always kidding.

Okay, Trips. I'm really, really sorry. I mean it. I shouldn't have shown up like that. But I'm tired of all this.

All what?

Of being your little secret. Why can't you tell them about me? About us?

So, that's what his stunt was all about. He wanted me to acknowledge our relationship.

Also, I badly wanted to see you, Rinks.

Whyyyyyyy?

Meet me and I'll tell you.

Fine, let's meet tomorrow. We should be home by lunch. Will give you a call.

Not tomorrow, Rinks. Tonight, now!

Zoinnnnng! Crazy excitement shot from my heart to all parts of my body. In a second, I'd gone from bristling babe to quivering kitten. Oh, gosh, just the thought of it!

Where are you staying? Text me the full address. I'll be there in ten.

I did. Then it hit me. OMG! OMG! I was going to meet Tejas, in Pondi, past curfew hours, while my friends slept. What is it about forbidden fruit that makes you want to sink your teeth in it?

Another bolt of realization hit me. The bike! He wouldn't just wake up my friends, he wouldn't just wake up the neighbours, he would wake up the dead!

TJ, wait, listen! Oh, shoot! Have you left already?

There was no reply for one whole minute.

Gotcha!

TJ could be such an ass.

Please tell me you're not coming on that bike.

Ok, I won't.

TJ! Please! I'm dead serious.

Relax, Rinks! I know the drill. Will park the car at the corner of the road.

Give me a missed call when you're here.

Yes, Ma'am. And Rinks, don't change.

Shucks, I hadn't thought about that.

I want to see you in that night suit you keep talking about. Bet you look super cute.

Ooooooh!

Just as well. There was no time to change. I ran to the washroom. Hurriedly brushed my teeth, sprayed on half a bottle of perfume, pulled my hair into a high pony, and stuffed my feet in a pair of flip-flops. All in record time.

I glanced back at Neha before softly letting myself out of the room. She was out like a light.

I was tiptoeing down the hall, holding out my hands in front of me when BUMPPPPPP!

Shit! Shit! Shit! I'd walked into someone! I let out a strangled scream.

A torch hit my eyes, blinding me for a second.

'Child, it is me, Jumbo.'

I nearly sank to my knees in relief. 'Mr Jumbo!'

'You no sleep?'

'Me no sleep. Me walk outside.'

'Okay, I come with you,' he said, shining the torch on himself.

Why on earth would I go for a moonlit walk with him?

'No, no, Mr Jumbo. Don't want to trouble you.'

'No trouble. Too much eating, too much gas. Walk good.'

Eww.

Beep! TJ had arrived! Oh, shoot!

Mr Jumbo was about to reach for the light switch.

'Look, Mr Jumbo,' I said hurriedly blocking his hand in some sort of a swift karate move. 'I need to be alone for some time. Why don't I give you fifty bucks? I'll go for a quick walk, be back in half an hour max.'

His eyebrows shot up.

'Twenty minutes max!'

I held my breath as he pondered over the offer.

'Hundred bucks, vokay?'

'Okay, okay! Tomorrow before leaving, promise. Please don't sleep off, stay right by the door. Will knock three times, okay?'

'Vokay.'

I shut the main door softly behind me and stepped out on to the cobblestoned street. TJ had parked a little distance away. My heart started doing some heavy duty aerobics.

I ran over to the passenger side. I was startled to find that somebody was already in there. I peered in. It was Pratyusha. My hand flew to my mouth. I was in my night suit. I'd no frickin' idea we'd have company.

But she was in no state to cluck at my sartorial choices, wrapped as she was all over her stupid boyfriend Arun. Who, by the way, was in the driver's seat. I squinted in the dark. There were two more people in the backseat as well. Bummer.

If TJ was planning to pull a Lord Shiva—show up with his uncouth hordes in tow—at least he could've given me an advance warning.

'Rinki, in here,' TJ whispered, opening the back door.

I dashed to the other side. Correction, there were *three* more people in the backseat. Shaina was on Deepak's lap, the two joined together at the hip and the mouth.

Before I could so much as mutter 'Get a room, guys', TJ scooped me into his arms.

'I missed you, Rinki,' he murmured in my hair. And for the next few minutes proceeded to show me just how much.

Having added to the Love Mobile's quota of steam

considerably, I was about to clamber out, when a cell's flash came on and Pesky Pratyusha slurred, 'Say cheese!'

You know that scene from horror movies where ghosts watch innocent folk while they sleep? Licking their lips, ready to feast on unsuspecting victims the moment their eyes open?

Yeah, so that's exactly what happened when I woke up the next day. Five ghouls were standing around the bed, frothing at the mouth, their eyes bloodshot. I let out a shriek before realizing the situation was way worse. One of them was waving a phone screen at my face. My blood went cold as I read the FB notification:

Pratyusha Raj tagged you in the photo titled 'Midnight drive with the lau birds at Pondi'.

The room erupted in a cacophony of screams.

'You are such a liar! Liar, liar, LIAR!'

'This is too much, even for you!'

'Care to explain?'

'What the hell's going on, Rinki?'

'What? When? Where? Why? How?'

Busted. Big time. What choice did I choice? I had to come clean with my friends. I sat them down and 'fessed up good and proper.

Told them everything. I mean, not everything. But you know, how it all started, where things stood, blah blah.

Robin was super pissed. She was acting as if I'd cheated on her with TJ. ('I can't look at your face right now.')

Sudha was more forgiving. ('It's okay, Rinki, try not to feel too guilty about it.')

Neha was ecstatic. ('We can go on double dates now.')

Google not so much. ('You can do better. What's so great about the guy, anyway?')

Adit looked as if he needed to talk to Ankita before airing his opinion.

I guess my friends needed time to process the information. They didn't talk to me all the way back to Chennai. But in time, like all good friends, they came around. Yay!

Epilogue

FYBC. First Year B.Com. One crazy year. Full of ups and downs. Waves and crests. Highs and lows.

On the downside:

I was a nobody at college.

Anks and I had fought big time.

I'd been ripped off by an unethical boss.

I'd met with a bike accident.

I'd tried to keep my love life under wraps and failed miserably. I mean, I was caught red-handed by my friends at Pondi.

Mom and Dad had briefly assumed that I was a goondi cum rowdy.

On the bright side:

I was making a name for myself at college. I was referred to as Gangster Rapper's best friend by teachers and classmates alike.

Anks and I'd made up. And we were closer than ever.

I'd made the creepy boss cough up the cash. Had promptly donated it to MSSF. Nope, that's not some NGO, that's Mom's

Silk Saree Fund. My parents must have done something really good to deserve a daughter like me, no?

I hadn't let the bike accident crush my spirits. Regrettably, the same could not be said of the mini bus driver's spirits. All thanks to my spitfire Mom.

I'd holidayed in Delhi with my friends, male pals included, without Mausiji and my other relatives being any the wiser.

I finally had a real-life, non-imaginary, gorgeous boyfriend.

What's more, I'd gone public with my relationship. I'm so glad I did. My new relationship status on FB drew over a hundred comments and God knows how many 'likes'.

The pluses outweighed the minuses.

It was all good. Life was going according to plan.

I was warming up to college. Oh yeah, I totally was.